P9-AZU-336

"You're making me nervous," Chrissy admitted. "What's going on?"

"Someone saw the notebook! Millie said she threw my stuff on the bed. The notebook was right on top of the laundry bag. Not inside of it. On top. It was probably right there on the bed, and while I was with Kevin, someone went in the room, read the notebook. That's why he burned the room!"

Chrissy gasped. "You're crazy. That's the weirdest thing I ever heard. Who would burn a room just because . . ."

"Because that person knows I'm getting closer. Maybe something in my notes hit on something. I was getting close, that much he knew. So he had to destroy the evidence."

"But all he had to do was steal it! He didn't have to burn down the room!" Chrissy protested.

"And risk getting caught with it later. Maybe he didn't have time to hide it. He heard someone coming. So he set it on fire and threw it in the wastebasket."

Chrissy, despite her earlier confidence, was finding herself being drawn into the theory. Something about it, as crazy as it sounded, was starting to make sense in a terrifying way.

"If that's true, then the person who did it knows you're on to something."

"Exactly." Angela was trembling. "That means," she said in a shaking voice, "sooner or later he has to make a move against me."

GLORIA GONZALEZ has written many scripts for television, as well as several plays. She lives in West New York, New Jersey.

ALSO AVAILABLE IN LAUREL-LEAF BOOKS:

AMULET OF DOOM, *Bruce Coville*
THE WARNING, *Amanda Byron*
THE HAUNTED DOLLHOUSE, *Susan Blake*
EVIL ON THE BAYOU, *Richie Tankersley Cusick*
FAMILY CRYPT, *Joseph Trainor*
DANCE OF DEATH, *Lou Kassem*
THE WATERY GRAVE, *Joseph Trainor*
STORM CHILD, *Susan Netter*
DRAWING THE DEAD, *Neil R. Selden*
SPIRITS AND SPELLS, *Bruce Coville*

QUANTITY SALES

Most Dell Books are available at special quantity discounts when purchased in bulk by corporations, organizations, and special-interest groups. Custom imprinting or excerpting can also be done to fit special needs. For details write: Dell Publishing Co., Inc., 1 Dag Hammarskjold Plaza, New York, NY 10017, Attn.: Special Sales Dept., or phone: (212) 605-3319.

INDIVIDUAL SALES

Are there any Dell Books you want but cannot find in your local stores? If so, you can order them directly from us. You can get any Dell book in print. Simply include the book's title, author, and ISBN number, if you have it, along with a check or money order (no cash can be accepted) for the full retail price plus 75¢ per copy to cover shipping and handling. Mail to: Dell Readers Service, Dept. FM, P.O. Box 1000, Pine Brook, NJ 07058.

A
Deadly
Rhyme

GLORIA GONZALEZ

Published by
Dell Publishing Co., Inc.
1 Dag Hammarskjold Plaza
New York, New York 10017

Copyright © 1986 by Gloria Gonzalez

All rights reserved. No part of this book may be reproduced or trans-
mitted in any form or by any means, electronic or mechanical, includ-
ing photocopying, recording or by any information storage and retrieval
system, without the written permission of the Publisher, except where
permitted by law.

Laurel-Leaf Library ® TM 766734, Dell Publishing Co., Inc.

Twilight(TM) is a trademark of Dell Publishing Co., Inc.

ISBN: 0-440-91866-9

RL: 7.0

Printed in the United States of America

October 1986

10 9 8 7 6 5 4 3 2 1

WFH

For Kelly who spent four years on the
mountain and inspired this tale

A
DEADLY
RHYME

One

GLENCORA.

The name sounded so pretty. It conjured up visions of mountain scenery, crushed autumn leaves, and brooks rushing between tall, sturdy trees.

The cover of the brochure featured a black and white photo, taken in winter, which showed the grounds buried under a white, lumpy blanket of snow. Laughing students, tossing snowballs, were shown against a background of front-porch dorms.

It was hard to believe that this paradise was just an hour and ten minutes from the heart of New York City.

"I know I'm going to hate boarding

1

school," Angela said, staring glumly out the car window. "I have a great idea! Let's turn around and go back home."

Her mother smiled. "Not a chance."

Okay. Angela had to admit that the mountain scenery of the past hour was spectacular. Not only had they seen DEER XING signs, but she'd actually spotted a deer transfixed, as if in a daze, near the edge of the road. The sprightly animal had sprung away before Angela could call out to her mother.

As they neared the mountaintop—and the school—Angela could feel her anxiety growing. Part of it had to do with leaving her friends behind, the prospects of being thrown in with a bunch of rich kids, but mostly it would mean the first time she would be separated from her mom.

"Look!" Carmela said.

Angela peered over the dashboard and saw the white wooden sign dangling on a rope, suspended from a fat tree:

GLENCORA
Est. 1843

"Kind of old, isn't it?" she moaned.

"Silly. That's what makes it so special," Carmela laughed. "I promise you, if you're unhappy here for half a second, I'll be right up to get you. Okay?"

"Okay," Angela nodded. The knot in her

stomach began to relax. Slightly. At that moment she resolved to make the best of the situation. It wasn't as if she'd never see her mother again.

Glencora had a liberal policy that encouraged weekend visits home twice a month if a student had good marks.

Carmela swung the car over the bumpy, hilly road and followed the markers to the lush soccer field now jammed with parked cars. Parents and students scurried about lugging suitcases, cardboard boxes, and assorted pieces of furniture. Angela noted the many out-of-state license plates, some from as far away as Nevada.

The campus seemed to be frozen in indecision between summer and autumn. While the grass was still thick and cushiony, the trees had begun to display more than a hint of orange and gold.

Carmela, reaching for the lever to open the car door, said brightly, "It's going to be okay. You'll see." For the first time Angela realized that the separation would be equally difficult for her mother. Maybe more so.

She braved a smile and stepped from the car just as a long, shiny gray limousine pulled alongside and parked. The uniformed driver held the door open for a blond girl in a white lace summer dress, who

3

clutched a small overnight bag and a ragged teddy bear. She strolled away as the chauffeur followed, carrying her luggage.

Carmela gasped. "I wonder who she is."

"With my luck—my roommate."

Carmela laughed and ran her fingers through her shoulder-length curly brown hair. She always did that when she was nervous, Angela knew. Standing there in her jeans, knee-high boots and jogging sweatshirt, Angela's mom could almost pass for one of the students.

A tall, lanky student wearing a football jersey raced over. "Hi. I'm Gary. And you are . . . ?"

"Angela. Angela Savino."

He consulted his clipboard and pointed them toward Maple House, one of the dorms at the top of the hill.

"You'll love it here," he said, grabbing up some of her luggage and leading them across the field. "I hated it at first too."

Carmela and Angela exchanged silent giggles behind his back.

"Is it that obvious?" Angela asked.

"Sure. You have that 'What am I doing here?' look. In a month you'll be finding excuses not to go home," he said, marching ahead.

"I doubt it," Angela mumbled.

Gary pointed out some of the campus

high spots: tennis courts, recreation building and student lounge, infirmary, gym, and the headmaster's house.

"The library is the only new building since the original school was built," Gary said, pointing to a futuristic glass-enclosed dome structure. "It was a gift from the estate of John Ambrose Blue."

"Who's he?" Angela asked.

"Only our most famous alumni. You never heard of him?"

Angela shrugged. "Nope."

"I know who he is," Carmela said. "He wrote all those ghost stories. We read him in high school. I remember reading the one about the man buried in the cellar."

"The Hangman's Tale," Gary offered.

"Right. For months I couldn't sleep with the lights off."

"He probably got those scary ideas from living here," Angela observed.

"Some people say he's never left," Gary said matter-of-factly.

Angela stopped in her tracks. "What?"

"Every once in a while someone claims to see his ghost prowling the campus at night." He smiled.

"You're kidding," Carmela gasped.

"Probably," Gary answered coolly.

"You ever see him?" Angela felt compelled to ask.

"Naw. But if I did, I wouldn't be scared. His legend is so strong here, I feel like I know him."

"Yeah. Well, I don't, and I don't particularly want to meet him," Angela said.

They quickly found themselves in front of the white two-story cottage encircled by a long, old-fashioned porch. The curtained windows sparkled against the afternoon sun. Inside, girls could be heard dashing up the stairs and opening and closing doors. Rock music blared from an open window.

"I'll tell Milli you're here," Gary said, depositing the luggage on the porch steps and disappearing into the house.

"Well," Carmela said, squeezing Angela's hand. "This is going to be your home for a while."

"Yeah. Me and the ghost."

"You're always dragging me to scary movies," Carmela said. "This should be right up your alley."

"Mom, I wanna go home."

"Honey, give it a chance. Look, we both decided this was the best thing."

Angela grunted. "You decided. I went along with it. Now I'm not so sure."

Carmela sat on the porch step. "You're getting older. I worry about you. I don't close up the restaurant till three in the morning. It's not fair to have you alone in

6

the apartment all those hours. It was all right when Grandma was with us, but now that she's gone . . . this school seems like the best idea."

Angela protested. "But when you're working it's not like I'm two blocks away or anything. We live right on top of the restaurant. I fall asleep listening to Mikey cleaning the pots in the kitchen. What am I going to hear in these woods at night? Ghosts and wild animals and wolves and deer! I'm not a country person."

"You'll get used to it. I did."

Angela and Carmela turned around and were confronted by a thin, smiling red-headed woman who extended her hand.

"Hi. I'm Millicent Greene. I'm your dorm parent and I teach art. Everyone calls me Milli. I'm from Atlanta, Georgia. Not a big city by New York standards, but I had great reservations about living so far away from anything. Now I love it. I think you will, too, Angela."

She had a pleasant voice that went with her friendly face. "I'll show you to your room."

Inside the house, parents and kids swarmed about, squeezing through the narrow carpeted corridors, lugging parcels, furniture, and clothes.

Milli surveyed the scene and shook her

7

head in displeasure. "We ask students not to bring too much initially, but every year they still arrive with their refrigerators, book-cases, and wicker chairs."

"Are refrigerators allowed?" Angela perked up, visions of midnight snacks looming ahead.

"It's not encouraged, but it's allowed. No hot plates, however, or any type of indoor cooking."

Angela's smile faded.

"But," she continued, as she paused to un-lock a room, "I have a hot plate and have been known to make great grilled cheese sandwiches—if you play your cards right. Now, this is your new home." Milli threw open the door to a large bare room that housed two beds, two desks, and a double closet with stacked pull-out drawers.

"All it needs is some personal touches and it'll be great," Carmela said, hoping Angela would catch her enthusiasm.

The most attractive feature was a large picture window that overlooked the woods.

"Try both beds and pick out the one you want before your roommate gets here," Mil-lie said. "I'll stop by before dinner and we can walk over together. If you need any-thing, rap on the wall. I'm right next door." She handed Angela the key to the room and left, closing the door behind her.

"I like her," Carmela said, as she slid clothes out of the suitcase and stacked them neatly on the bed.

Angela didn't hear her. She was concentrating on an elderly man, bundled in a dark coat, who was hurrying through the woods. Something in his manner, in his quick movements, aroused her curiosity. Her gaze followed him down a dirt path that seemed to dip off the face of the earth. She made a mental note to see where the road led to.

A quick knock on the door interrupted Angela's thoughts. Carmela opened the door to find the limousine driver and his blond charge framed in the doorway.

"I believe this is my room," the girl said, without any particular enthusiasm.

"Come in, come in," Carmela urged.

The girl glanced about, nodded in Angela's direction, and deposited her bag on the unoccupied bed.

"My name is April," she announced as the driver brought in her bags.

Before Angela could respond, the girl proclaimed, "I don't like loud music, so if you play your stereo, I would appreciate it if you'd use earphones. I like my privacy, so if you intend to entertain friends, I hope you will limit their visits. I like things to look neat, and I intend to keep my half of the room spotless. I don't borrow clothes or makeup, nor do I lend them. I know we'll get along." She breezed out the door.

"April," Angela yelled at the departing blond head.

"Yes?" the girl turned and smiled sweetly.

"I didn't bring my stereo, I don't have any friends, I wear very little makeup, and your clothes wouldn't fit me. Besides, I rarely wear dresses. And if you want to get along with me, don't give me orders."

"I'll keep that in mind," the girl responded.

"Do that," Angela said, as she began hanging up her clothes.

For the first time, after almost nine months of planning, Carmela had second thoughts about leaving her daughter in the school.

As if reading her mind, Angela smiled at her mother: "It's okay. It's going to take more than a ghost and a wacko roommate to get me to quit."

Two

Dear Mom,

I'm writing this from English class. Mr. Slavin thinks I'm working on a composition about my worldly ambitions.

It turns out April isn't as strange and mean as I thought. This will really knock you out—her mother is Casey Elliot, the blond in the TV series about police-women. At her last school the kids teased April about her mother being a dumb actress—and then that sexy poster came out and it didn't help. I'm the only one she's told, and that's only because I saw Casey's picture fall out of a book, where April hides them. She's really crazy about her

11

mom and misses her. They call each other twice a week. I told her to be proud, put the pictures on her desk, and if anyone says anything to tell them off!

It really gets cold up here on this mountain at night, and I sleep with a sweater over my pajamas and socks on my feet. April's mom sent her an electric blanket— that's a hint.

Love,
Angela

Dear Baby,
Glad you liked the blanket. Mikey and the waiters send their love, as do the regulars. Everyone is impressed that you're at private school. They didn't even complain when I raised the menu prices.

Be patient with April. The rich have problems too (though I can't imagine what they could be).

What are your teachers like?

Love,
Mom

Dear Mom:
Someone broke into the gym last night and wrote "The end is near" all over the walls. Headmaster Norseworthy addressed the whole school at morning

meeting and said he'll suspend whoever did it.

The janitor, Mr. Neely, had to ride into town today to buy paint, and April and I went along. We had pizza while he went to the hardware store. His wife is the school's cook, and their son, Kevin, is the captain of the football team. He's also in the photography club, which I'm thinking of joining. He has blond hair and blue-green eyes, and so far he doesn't know I exist. I hope to change that.

The other excitement was that Mr. Shulte, the drama teacher, got sick during dinner and they had to take him to the hospital. He was back in school today, but he still looks kind of pale. He's making jokes about being "poisoned."

You'd like him. He's funny, and always wears a baseball cap, and he and Milli are engaged. Sometimes when I go into her room at night for a cup of hot chocolate— or whatever new recipe she's experimenting with—he'll join us.

Señor Flores is upset because I'm not picking up Spanish. He says it should be easy since I'm Italian, but I told him I don't understand Italian either.

Most of the teachers are nice. Every night at dinner we sit at different tables,

*with a different teacher. There are seven
students to each table.*

Last night I sat with Mrs. Portnoy, the
math teacher, who talked about all her
illnesses. She also claims to have seen the
ghost of John Ambrose Blue drinking
from the water fountain at the soccer field
a few weeks ago. She's around a hundred
years old. She still isn't used to girls being
at the school. Did I tell you, there are only
twelve of us? The thirteenth girl is regis-
tered but hasn't shown up yet. For some
reason everyone is very mysterious about
her.

I'm not sure that Mrs. Portnoy likes the
idea of girls being enrolled, but Mr.
Shulte is thrilled. He says he can finally
cast the school plays with female students
instead of women teachers.

Tonight I'll be sitting with Mr. Theopopolis, the history teacher. He's about
150 years old with fat, white eyebrows
and white hair. He looks like the mad sci-
entist in all those scary movies. Kids make
fun of him, but actually he's become my
favorite teacher. I look forward to going
to class. History doesn't have to be boring,
I realized, if the person teaching it loves
the subject. I volunteered to help him
with his filing. We get extra marks for
serving as a teacher's assistant and even

though he says very little, I know he likes me. Yesterday I gave him a small plant to put on his desk, and for the first time I actually saw him smile. Not a big smile, because he turned it off as soon as he noticed that I noticed him smiling, but I could tell he was touched.

Miss Dixon, the music teacher, is also ancient, but she acts younger than everyone. Her boyfriend is the funeral director in town, and sometimes he picks her up in the hearse. She thinks its fun.

Mr. Rome, the athletic director, is the campus Romeo. His wife, who teaches biology, is very quiet. They are truly an odd couple.

Then there's Mr. Lang, the science teacher, who spends class time talking about sports or movies. He doesn't get along with the headmaster, but his students keep winning prizes for science projects, so I guess they can't fire him. The kids love him.

Last week as a class assignment he put these names on the blackboard: Henry Kissinger, Babe Ruth, Winston Churchill, Dr. Salk, and Pope John XXIII.

He said, "Assuming all these people lived at the same time, each was critically ill, and you had only enough serum to save one, which one would you save?"

Let me tell you, the answers were pretty wild. Oh, we were also allowed to write in the name of one celebrity. You know who got the most votes? Clint Eastwood! So much for a private school education!

By the way, Nurse Samuels had me up in the infirmary yesterday to type and file reports. Every week we're assigned to different duties. Next week I have kitchen detail, which I'm not looking forward to, except that Kevin often comes in to help his mom clean up after meals.

Have to go.

I'm trying out for the school play.

Love,
Angela

Glencora
Glenwell on the Hudson, New York

Dear Parents:

There was an incident at the school last week in which a person or persons broke into the infirmary. Valuable equipment and furniture was destroyed. The pharmaceutical cabinet, which is locked at all times, was broken into, and its contents rifled. Many medical records were also removed, so we ask that parents send us copies of their children's medical history so we can replace our files.

It was a regrettable incident, and a

campus investigation is under way. The local police are cooperating with us in this matter.

Horton Norseworthy
Headmaster

Dear Mom:
Big excitement here today. Girl number 13 finally arrived—by helicopter! It landed right in the middle of the soccer field during practice.

Even the headmaster and Nurse Samuels came running over to watch the people get out of the plane.

The girl and her father—and some other men in foreign uniforms—were taken to the administration building.

It turns out the girl, Selena, is the daughter of King Elizzaroes, who rules some island near Greece. That makes her a real-life princess!

Oh, a scary thing happened last night. I was walking back to the dorm after play rehearsal and it was very dark. Not even a star in the sky. And cold. We had snow-flakes earlier in the evening. Suddenly I had the feeling someone was following me. I turned around quickly, and I saw something running toward the trees. I ran and didn't stop till I got into my room.

17

*April said it was probably a deer. I guess
so.*

*The play is next week. Don't expect too
much—no one knows their lines.*
Bring food!

Love,
Angela

Three

The play had gone smoothly. Two props were knocked over, a few lighting cues were missed, and one of the students occasionally forgot his lines. Still, the audience gave the cast resounding applause.

Angela's lines, which consisted of "Dinner is served" and "Someone from Scotland Yard to see you," had been delivered flawlessly.

As the cast assembled onstage for photos, student waiters walked among the parents dispensing glasses of champagne.

"You must be Angela's mother," a grinning man said to Carmela.

"Yes. How did you know?"

"She told me to look for the prettiest woman."

Carmela looked down at the bubbles in her glass. Any compliment unnerved her.

He held out his hand. "I'm Bob Shulte, drama coach."

"Then you're to be congratulated. The play went beautifully."

Mr. Shulte glanced across the room, and the expression on his face swiftly changed. Carmela followed his gaze and saw Mr. Norseworthy walking toward them. She had forgotten how handsome and elegant the headmaster was. In his gray blazer and blue slacks he could easily pass for an older male model.

"Nice to have met you," Mr. Shulte said before turning and walking quickly away.

"Mrs. Savino! I can't tell you what a delight it is having Angela with us. She's a very special child," Mr. Norseworthy said, clutching her arm above the elbow. "We like to get the parents involved in our campus activities. Perhaps some Friday night you'll attend one of our career seminars and talk to the students about the restaurant business."

Carmela shrugged. "It would probably bore them."

"Not at all. We have two seniors planning to attend culinary college and one wants to operate his father's chain of hotels. Please try to come."

She found herself agreeing. "All right."

Mr. Norseworthy's wife rushed over to say he was needed onstage with the cast. They excused themselves and hurried away.

Before Carmela could move, a voice whispered from behind, "I was hoping to have a moment with you." Carmela spun around and found herself facing an elderly man wearing thick bifocals. "It's about Angela," he said somberly.

"You must be Mr. Theopopolis."

"Yes, I'm her history teacher."

Carmela smiled. "She's spoken of you many times. I'm very happy to meet you."

He didn't appear to notice she had extended her hand. He looked quickly about the room. Parents were talking and laughing in little groups. He leaned closer, and she could sense that something was troubling him.

"I'm not sure she's safe here," the man told her.

The words had come so quickly that she wasn't sure she had heard correctly.

"I'm sorry, I didn't . . ."

The old man turned away before she could finish. She watched him weave through the crowd and disappear, just as Angela rushed toward her.

"You were wonderful!" Carmela said, cupping her daughter's chin and looking into the big, hazel eyes framed by the long strands of chestnut hair. That smile, with a devilish dimple crinkling each cheek, was her greatest attribute.

"Wasn't that the worst play ever?" Angela confided.

"The pits," her mother whispered. "But you saved it."

"Come on," Angela said, grabbing her mother's hand and leading her quickly toward the exit.

"Where are we going?"

"You'll see."

Within moments they were outside in the cold air. The campus was dark and silent except for the howling of a dog somewhere in the woods.

"Sounds like a wolf," her mother said, pushing her coat collar high against her neck.

"Wild dogs. There's a whole pack of them living on the mountain. They don't bother us unless they're hungry. Sometimes at night they come down and turn over the garbage cans."

A biting cold wind whipped her coat open as she struggled to keep pace with Angela.

"Are we almost there?"

"Almost."

Amber beacons, encased in small steel-ribbed cages, stood inches off the ground, illuminating the paths between the cottages and the campus buildings. The golden glow, while lovely, gave little light.

Angela bolted off the main path, crushing Carmela's hopes that they were headed to her cottage. She could feel her face stinging from the wind.

"Do you walk around here alone at night?"

"Sure. First couple of times it was scary, but you get used to it."

Carmela was certain she would never get used to it. Still, she was secretly proud that Angela had not inherited her fear of darkness and the outdoors.

Miles away, a single car wound its way slowly up the mountain, its red taillights gleaming like bats' eyes. A yellow half-moon hung above the naked tree branches, making them appear to be long, protruding black fingers.

The campus was far behind them as they began a slow decline down a hill thick with bushes. Off to the side could be heard the rumblings of an angry brook.

"Angela, this is crazy!" Carmela exclaimed. "Let's go back. We'll do it some other time."

"Just a few more feet," Angela said. "You can make it."

Carmela, unable to see more than an arm's length in front of her, grabbed on tightly to Angela's sleeve. She almost stumbled to her knees when Angela suddenly came to an abrupt halt.

"What is it?" the mother asked nervously.

"We're here," Angela told her.

"Where?" Carmela shivered.

"Look."

Carmela leaned forward and squinted. All she saw was a pile of rocks.

"You brought me here, in the middle of the woods, to look at rocks?"

Angela took her hand and led her closer, within inches of the find.

Carmela took a closer look and gasped. "A cemetery!"

"Give me a match," Angela said. "You have to see this."

Carmela fumbled in her purse, unable to get her frozen fingers to move rapidly. "I'm not sure I want to."

Angela quickly struck a match and crouched down on her knees. She held the tiny flame over the granite headstone that swelled from the ground.

"What does it say?" Carmela whispered.

Angela moved the flame slightly over the carving dug into the headstone:

R
1870–1923

The wind blew out the match and Angela quickly lighted another one, holding it cupped in her palm over the second stone:

S
1890–1923

Carmela found another pack of matches, struck one, and held it aloft near the third stone:

J
1911–1923

"What do you think it means?" Angela asked.

"I have no idea," Carmela said, unable to stop looking at the three headstones, which seemed to sag toward the ground.

"There's not another grave anywhere else in the woods," Angela said excitedly. "Just these three. Why here?"

"I know one thing . . ." Carmela trembled, and she wasn't sure it was just because of the cold.

"What?"

"The three of them died together."

"That's what I figured," Angela said quickly.

The match blew out just as a twig snapped behind them. Turning toward the sound, they caught sight of a tall figure racing between the trees.

Carmela screamed and threw Angela to the ground.

Four

Milli chuckled. "Of course it was a deer," she said.

They sat in her room sipping hot chocolate from blue porcelain mugs decorated with tiny Dutch windmills.

"It looked like a man to me," Carmela said, happily bundled in a woolen shawl, with her feet tucked snugly under a needlepoint pillow.

"The ghost of John Ambrose Blue?" Milli's eyes twinkled with mischief.

Carmela did not respond to the intended joke.

"I'm sorry," the teacher said. "Obviously, something did frighten you both. It's just that when I first came here all I heard about was the ghost on the mountain, and for a while I wasn't sure if it was true or not."

"Did you ever see it?" Angela asked.

"Don't be silly. There's no ghost."

"Mrs. Portnoy said she saw him drinking from the water fountain. She told me," Angela said.

Milli, dressed in a full-length pink robe, got up and took the teakettle to refill their cups.

"Mrs. Portnoy is a very capable teacher— a gentle, lovely woman—but she has a slight problem."

"You mean, she's . . . nuts?" Angela asked.

"She drinks."

Carmela sighed.

"Not a lot. Never when she has a class in the morning. But she is known to tie one on now and then."

Outside, a gust of wind rattled the windows. Carmela glanced at the ceramic clock on the bookcase and noted unhappily that it was almost midnight.

"I should be heading home soon."

"I wish I could invite you to stay the night, but I'm afraid it's against school policy," Milli said.

"She could sleep in my bed. I could sneak

her out before breakfast," Angela said quickly.

"Honey, I can't. I have to be at the fish market before dawn or we won't have any seafood on the menu." They were interrupted by a knock on the door. Milli opened the door to admit Selena.

"I can't find my math book. Is it okay if I go over to Jane's dorm and borrow hers?" she asked.

Miss Grove smiled but said, "No. It is not okay."

"Then I'll fail the test tomorrow."

"Should have thought about it earlier," Milli replied. The dark-haired girl flashed an angry look and stormed from the room.

"Beautiful girl," Carmela observed.

"The boys would certainly agree with you," Milli said. "At first the kids seemed afraid of her because of the poem. But they soon got over it."

"What poem?" Carmela asked.

"Didn't I tell you?" Angela squealed.

"I don't remember."

"I thought I wrote you about it. The whole thing is so dumb, but that's all anybody here talks about. You can't get through a day without hearing about John Ambrose Blue. It's all very boring, if you ask me." She yawned. The combination of the hot drink and the soft steam heat whistling through the pipes was the perfect inducement to sleep.

"The poem is certainly one of his lesser works," Milli said. "In fact, he probably would have destroyed it after he became famous, but my guess is he had forgotten that he'd written it."

"I read a few of his stories, but I don't remember any poem," Carmela said.

"You haven't missed anything," Angela said, stretching out on the couch with her head on her mother's lap.

"You have to admit, whether you like the poem or not, it's a strange coincidence," said Milli.

Carmela noted the hint of apprehension in her voice. It hadn't been there moments ago. She found herself suddenly growing nervous. "Will someone tell me what we're talking about?"

Milli crossed the room and removed a faded, coffee-brown leather volume from the bookcase. "Eighty years ago, John Ambrose Blue was a student here. He didn't stand out as anyone special. No one paid any mind to his boasts of being a famous writer one day. Just as well, or the school would have saved every piece of paper he ever doodled on.

"But he did become internationally

known for his novels, and when they were remodeling the original cottage, they discovered an old notebook of his, which contained the poem."

Carmela shrugged. "Is it so unusual for a student to write about his schooldays?"

Milli moved closer. "His poem tells of the destruction of the school."

"Read it to her," Angela suggested, stretching out on the couch.

"Please," Carmela added, suddenly finding herself drawn to the mystery.

Milli took the book and resumed her seat on the overstuffed chair. She read in a soft voice:

"Glencora
"And so as night must come to pass,
  And shadows fall among us all,
'Tis time to sing a silent mass
  Of terrors that the soul does pall.

"Glencora's name in blood is writ,
  The flames the very stars will touch.
And those whose eyes behold the shame
  Will henceforth quiver to the name . . .
    Glencora.

"On such an eve of crimson red,
  The graves will shake and spill their dead,

A ghostly dance of nocturnal noises—
  And not a witness shall survive its
     voices.

"And so my students, heed my call,
  The shadows will forecast the fall.
A kingly visit to herald the lights,
  A somber duel of silent knights.

"A stranger will trod the weary path,
  Her very being arousing the wrath,
The sins of fathers on all will rain,
  Their bloody deeds, the work of Cain.

"A parting thought for those that care,
  For I, you see, will not be there.
Enjoy the rainbow daylight hours,
  But commence to flee upon the showers.

"And when upon the hill you gaze,
  The cinders of her ashen days,
Remember when she is no more,
  I warned you thus . . . a mere
     fourscore."

Milli closed the book and handed it to Angela.

"What does it mean?" Carmela asked. "It's all so vague."

"When he wrote this, eighty years ago, Glencora was strictly a male military academy," said Milli. "Yet he predicted that girls

would attend: 'A stranger will trod the path
—her.' "

"Maybe he meant a woman teacher."

"They had a woman teacher when he was
a student. Mrs. Theopopolis, who taught
Latin. But this is the first year that the school
has admitted female students."

"Sounds farfetched."

"True," Milli agreed, "but what do you
make of his prediction—'a kingly visit'?"

"Selena's father is a king, and he did visit
the school," Angela said, "but I think it's just
a coincidence. And the poem is still dumb."

Milli smiled. "And," she said, "it is way
past all our bedtimes."

"Yes," Carmela said, reaching for her
coat. "Thanks for the hot chocolate and entertainment."

"My pleasure."

Angela took the book and strode across
the room to replace it on the shelf. She was
just about to close it when an inscription on
the first page caught her eye:

To Milli
My very best,
H.N.

It wasn't Mr. Shulte's initials, and she wondered who had given Milli the book. Proba-

bly some relative, she thought as she placed it on the shelf.

"Tuck me in, Mom?"

"Sure."

Carmela and Angela said good-night to Milli and tiptoed next door to Angela's room.

They opened the door softly so as not to awaken April, but she bolted to a sitting position as they entered. "I was getting worried. I didn't know what happened to you."

"We were with Milli," Angela said, digging in her dresser for her pajamas.

"You missed all the excitement," April said.

"I don't think so," Carmela said. "We had plenty of our own."

"I meant Miss Dixon."

"What happened to her?" Angela asked.

"A bunch of us were walking from the auditorium after the play when Gary came running over. He was on his way to get Nurse Samuels. He'd found Miss Dixon lying on the ground."

"Who?" Carmela asked.

"Dixon, the music teacher," Angela said quickly. "Then what?"

"They carried her up to the infirmary, and it turns out she had fainted. Gary thought she was dead. It really scared him."

"I bet."

"But you know what she said when she came to? She said she'd seen him."

Angela was afraid she already knew the answer but asked the question anyway: "Who did she see?"

April whispered, "The ghost of John Ambrose Blue."

Angela and her mother exchanged worried glances.

"She swears she saw him," April insisted. "She knows it was him because he was wearing the blue cape, just like in the picture that's in his book. He was running across the field and went right past her. That's all she remembers, because she fainted."

"How many people know about this?" Angela asked.

"Just the few of us who were there, but by tomorrow it'll be all over the campus."

Carmela lingered in the room, making sure the girls were sufficiently calm before she left. She had offered to stay, but Angela wouldn't hear of it.

"Mom, you're being silly," she insisted. "There's no such thing as ghosts. You told me that yourself."

Carmela tucked them in, kissed Angela, and closed the door softly behind her.

Outside the cottage the cold wind slammed against her as she hurried to the car parked a few feet away on the lawn. She was reaching for the door handle when a piece of paper on the windshield caught her attention.

She was tempted to ignore the paper, but she reached over the ice-crusted windshield and yanked it free from the grip of the wiper. She was about to crumple it into a ball when she saw what appeared to be a message saying "Get it out." Annoyed, she tossed the paper to the ground and hurried into her car.

She started the engine and pulled away thinking, "If parking isn't allowed here, they should put up a sign, not just put a note on a person's windshield."

Had it not been so cold, had she not been so concerned about getting home, had the moon been a little brighter, had she taken just another moment, she might have read the note more carefully.

As she drove along, she began to wonder if she had misread the note. She was sorry she had thrown it away. She was no longer sure whether it said "Get *it* out" or "Get *her* out."

Five

Angela sat in class and wondered unhappily what the ancient Incas had to do with her plans to be a fashion designer. Mr. Theopopolis drew a map on the green chalkboard and droned on about the mysteries of the pre-Columbian civilization.

A seat away, Selena was bent over her notebook drawing hearts pierced with arrows. April had her book propped open on her desk as she polished her nails behind it.

Angela glanced across the aisle at her new friend Chrissy, who appeared to be taking notes on the lecture, but was actually writing in her diary. Angela found herself smiling. In the past few days she had gotten to know the girl and felt closely drawn to her quiet ways. Like herself, Chrissy was somewhat of an outsider. Shy, preferring books to people, she would never make the most-popular list. Yet she was bright and sensible and had a zany sense of humor—when she chose to display it. Chrissy caught Angela's glance and winked.

Outside the window the trees stood stiffly, arrayed in the brilliant reds and oranges of the season. Soon snow would cover the mountaintop. Angela had to admit she had fallen under the spell of Glencora's rustic setting.

A piece of paper sailed past her desk and slid to the floor. Angela quickly scooped it up and read the handwritten message: "Will you go to the Halloween dance with me?" It was signed "Kevin."

Angela turned and glanced at the blond-haired boy sitting two rows away, with his long legs stretched out on the aisle. He grinned, and she grinned back.

After class, as she and Chrissy walked slowly toward the library, Kevin ran toward them and blocked their path.

"Will you?" he asked.

"Maybe," Angela smiled. Chrissy mumbled something about meeting her later and continued walking.

"Please," Kevin persisted.

She had never been this close to him before. Their conversation was usually a "Hi" as he dashed through the school hall. In her neighborhood he would be the catch of the year. She wondered why Selena hadn't snapped him up.

However flattered, she was still a realist. "Why me?"

He grinned. "Because I suspect you're the only girl in the whole school with a sense of humor. And—" He stared down at the ground, and for the first time Angela realized that the gorgeous star athlete was shy.

"And?" she asked.

"I'm thinking of going as Popeye, 'cause I can borrow my dad's navy uniform, and I think we could win if you went with me as Sweet Pea."

Angela groaned. "Do I have to wear a diaper?" No matter how popular and good-looking he was, there were limits!

"The prize for best couple is a hundred dollars. I sure could use half of that." He looked like a little boy pleading for a cookie. Somehow she found it utterly appealing.

"What would you do with the money?"

His voice rose with excitement. "Mr. Rome has a 35-mm camera he's selling for forty-five dollars. A new one would cost a couple of hundred. Would take me years to save up." He dug his hands deeper into his pockets. "Pretty dumb idea, huh?"

She allowed his anxiety to grow and then responded softly. "No, it's not."

He grinned. "You'll do it!"

"Where am I going to get a diaper to fit me?"

"Easy. I'll borrow a white tablecloth from the kitchen."

Angela's smile faded. "I'll have to go in front of the whole school wearing a tablecloth?"

"And a baby bonnet," he said quickly. "But think—you'll have fifty dollars and a trophy. Please."

Before she realized it, she was saying "Okay" and he was hugging her excitedly. "Meet me in the rec hall after study." Before she could respond, he dashed off, waving.

In the library Chrissy listened to Angela's story and after sorting the details offered her opinion: "You did the right thing."

"You sure?"

"Positive."

Chrissy returned her attention to the books in front of her and Angela felt a warm glow. That's what she liked about her new friend. She had a no-nonsense approach to life and yet a relaxed, easy-going attitude.

40

Angela hoped it would somehow rub off on her.

They parted at the entrance to the cottage and Chrissy walked down the corridor to her room at the other end of the house. She found Selena and April sitting on the floor giggling. Her happiness faded. Selena had been hanging around April constantly, and Angela had detected a new aloofness from her roommate. Besides, they always appeared to be involved in some type of conspiracy.

"See you later," Selena said, jumping to her feet and dashing out the door.

"Lovely manners," Angela mumbled, throwing her books on the bed.

"She's okay when you get to know her," April said, somewhat coolly. "Kevin Neely said he has basketball practice, so if he's late, wait for him."

"Thank you," Angela said, gathering her shampoo and towels.

"Why are you meeting Kevin? Does he need help with his homework?" April asked, a bit too sweetly.

"No."

April persisted. "It can't be a date. He doesn't date anyone. Everyone's tried and given up chasing him. Selena even signed up for photography just to be in his class. I

41

know—he's interviewing you for the school paper. Right?"

Angela smiled. "Wrong." She grabbed her soap and headed out of the room. Pausing in the doorway, she struck a dramatic pose. "If Kevin stops by, tell him I'm in the shower and I'll call him later."

Angela knew that before she could turn on the hot water tap April would run to Selena's room with the news of her "date."

Her prediction proved correct. Hours later, seated at dinner, Chrissy leaned over and whispered, "I hear you and Kevin are really *serious.*"

"Who said?"

Chrissy busied herself tossing her salad. "Janie, Nancy, Ruth, Hector, Bobby . . ."

Angela gasped. "You're kidding!"

Chrissy tried to keep a straight face but found it difficult. "Suddenly I'm the friend of a celebrity," she said with a laugh.

"April!" Angela fumed.

"That's not all I found out," Chrissy told her. "You remember that dumb pirate movie that April's mother was in?"

Angela nodded. The class had been allowed to miss study hall in order to watch the television movie.

"Well, she's sending April the pirate outfit and she's going to the Halloween party as

Peter Pan and Selena will be Captain Hook."

Angela's heart sank. She could see Kevin's camera flying out the window.

"They already have the prize money spent," Chrissy said, not bothering to conceal her annoyance.

Angela groaned.

"Anything wrong?" Mr. Slavin asked from across the table.

"No," Angela perked up. "Everything's fine."

The teacher then resumed his conversation about the merits of film versus theater. Chrissy and Angela pretended to be interested. Two tables away, Milli and Mr. Shulte seemed to be enjoying a private joke. This was in sharp contrast to Mr. and Mrs. Rome, at a nearby table, who seemed to be glaring at each other. At the headmaster's table, Mr. Norseworthy was in a deep conversation with Selena. His wife, sitting with Nurse Samuels, chatted away with the students.

Gary approached Angela's table and placed water glasses in front of all the diners. Before his hasty departure, he leaned over and whispered—but loudly enough for all to hear—"Kevin said don't forget."

Angela said, grinning, "Kevin who?"

The mood was broken by Jed Hart, the admissions director, who screamed, "Watch out!" All eyes turned to his table. As they did so, the overhead chandelier crashed to the floor, narrowly missing Jed's companion.

Señor Flores sat rigid, his clothes covered with plaster, as a thin trail of blood oozed down his cheek.

Six

After lunch on Saturday, Angela and Chrissy rode into town with Mrs. Rome, who was headed for the beauty parlor. The biology teacher refused to divulge details of her costume for the Halloween party but hinted her hairdo would play a major role.

She dropped the girls off at the pizza store in the shopping mall, saying "Pick you up in two hours."

Armed with money from home, the girls ate a quick lunch and headed for the cosmetic counter of the department store.

"I never use that stuff," Chrissy said, overwhelmed by the wide assortment of lipsticks, blushers, and eye shadows.

"Never too late to start," Angela said, using the sample cosmetics to give her friend an instant makeover.

"I feel dumb," Chrissy complained. Angela ignored her and continued brushing a light blue powder over her eyelids.

The saleslady asked crisply, "Can I help you?"

Angela smiled. "No, we're doing fine."

Chrissy grumbled, "Speak for yourself."

A few minutes later the lip gloss in place, Angela stepped back to admire her work. "Beautiful," she exclaimed.

She pointed Chrissy toward a mirror on the counter.

"What do you think?"

Chrissy stared at herself for a long time. Was that really her? The makeup, applied so lightly as to be almost unnoticeable, still brought out the color of her hazel eyes, and her pale skin now had a vibrant glow.

"I love it!" she found herself admitting.

"Good," Angela beamed. "We'll take one of each," Angela told the salesgirl as she pushed the samples across the counter.

"I can't let you pay for all that," Chrissy protested.

"I'll be using it too," Angela assured her.

They spent the next two hours browsing through the various stores and looking at the latest fashions. At the ice cream parlor,

Chrissy treated Angela to a giant chocolate milkshake. They invested two dollars in quarters in a video game and then headed back to meet Mrs. Rome.

For Angela it was the best day she had spent since leaving home. The costume party later that night would be the icing on the cake.

While they waited for the teacher, Angela dug her mother's letter out of her purse and read it to Chrissy.

Dear Baby,

We had some excitement of our own here the other night. The oven caught fire and we managed to get all the people out before the firemen arrived. No one was hurt.

The damage was confined to the kitchen, and we had to close the restaurant for three days while we cleaned and painted. The walls are now bright yellow. You'll love it.

The best thing about the fire (didn't I tell you every dark cloud has a silver lining?) was meeting Dixie, one of the firemen. He comes from South Carolina and has a slight southern accent. His real name is Bill but everyone calls him Dixie.

He stopped by yesterday on his day off to help us paint and stayed for lunch.

Guess what? He's taking me to the movies tonight.

Love,
Mom

P.S. *Your new friend Chrissy sounds very nice. I knew you'd find someone special. Can't wait to meet her."*

Chrissy didn't need any blusher. Her cheeks were glowing. "That's nice," she smiled.

A car horn tooted and the girls walked toward Mrs. Rome's station wagon. They jumped into the car, noticing that the woman was wearing a heavy scarf over her head.

"Can't we see your hair?" Angela asked.

"Not till tonight," the teacher said, "when I'm in full costume."

Angela suddenly thought of the stupid, frilly baby bonnet she would be wearing and wondered if Kevin was worth it. She decided, without much debate, that he was.

Back at the school, Mrs. Rome dropped them off by the gym as she went in to find her husband. Angela and Chrissy hurried across the soccer field and suddenly spotted the ambulance parked in front of their cottage.

"What could it be?" Angela asked nervously. The girls walked faster.

The ambulance was surrounded by silent students.

Angela darted through the crowd and entered the house just as two uniformed attendants hurried past bearing a stretcher.

She glanced down at the still form strapped beneath the gray blanket. It was Milli. Her eyes were closed.

Within moments, sirens blaring, the ambulance raced down the mountain with Mr. Shulte accompanying Milli.

"She's going to be okay. Just had the wind knocked out of her," a voice told Angela. "She slipped and hit her head."

She spun around and faced Kevin. "How do you know?"

"I'm a reporter," he smiled. "I asked the ambulance driver."

Selena rushed over. "I was the one who found her. I called the ambulance."

Angela groaned inwardly. Of all people.

"What happened to her?" Chrissy asked.

"I was ironing my costume and I took the iron to the bathroom to fill it with water and just before I went in I heard a scream and found Miss Green on the floor. I went in and almost slipped. I practically landed on top of her. Then I ran and got Nurse Samuels, and she told me to call the hospital."

Angela sat quietly while Selena rambled

on about how upset Mr. Shulte had been when Jed told him.

Selena spotted April and dashed off to join her, enjoying her new celebrity status.

"I'm going to the hospital. I'll see you later," Kevin said.

Angela walked slowly to her room, frowning.

Chrissy followed her. "What's wrong?"

"I'm not sure," Angela replied, still deep in thought.

"Come on," she told Chrissy, leading her down the carpeted hall to the bathroom. She opened the door and closed it as soon as Chrissy entered behind her. Selena's iron was still on the floor where she had dropped it. Angela bent down and examined the tile floor.

"What are you looking for?" Chrissy whispered.

Angela moved her fingers slowly along the floor. She motioned to Chrissy. "Come here and feel this," she said. Chrissy bent down and touched the floor.

"What do you feel?" Angela asked.

"I'm not sure. Something sticky."

"Right," said Angela. She sniffed her fingers. Whatever the substance was, it was colorless and odorless. "Vaseline?"

Chrissy nodded. "Could be. What are you getting at?"

"This was no accident," Angela told her. "Let's go to my room."

Both were relieved to find the room empty. Selena's Captain Hook costume, with the purple plumed hat, was placed neatly on the bed next to April's Peter Pan outfit.

"What made you suspect something was wrong?" Chrissy asked, sitting on the bed.

"Selena said she slipped when she walked into the bathroom. Kevin said Milli slipped. In the two months that we've been here, have you heard of anyone slipping in the bathroom?"

Chrissy said she hadn't.

"Then why two people within minutes?"

"You mean that someone put the stuff there on purpose so Milli would fall?"

"Sure looks that way," Angela said.

"But she could've been killed!"

"Exactly."

Chrissy bolted from the bed and headed toward the door.

"Where are you going?"

"To tell Mr. Norseworthy. If there's a maniac running around, he should be told."

"You can't tell him," Angela stopped her.

"Why not?"

"Because," Angela said calmly, "it could be him."

Seven

An hour later Chrissy and Angela were huddled over a stack of books in the library. The large reading room was empty except for the librarian, who busied herself stacking books from the wooden cart.

"What exactly are we looking for?" Chrissy asked.

"I'm not sure," Angela said, thumbing through the various school yearbooks.

"Great," Chrissy said, throwing open yet another book written by John Ambrose Blue. She skimmed the pages with little enthusiasm.

"Someone connected to the school is out to destroy it. Maybe there's a clue here somewhere," said Angela, reaching for another book.

"Maybe Milli just tripped."

Angela closed the book hard. "And maybe the chandelier just 'happened' to fall. Maybe Mr. Shulte just ate something that didn't agree with him. Maybe someone broke into the infirmary for fun. Maybe a ghost wrote 'The end is near' on the walls." She shook her head. "Too many maybes."

Chrissy smiled. "Maybe."

"And maybe that was a deer I saw out in the cemetery."

"Probably," her friend said. "Why would someone want to destroy the school? And even if they had a grudge against it, why take it out on Milli and Mr. Shulte and Señor Flores? It doesn't make sense."

"Can you explain all these things that have happened?" Angela asked her.

"No. Not really. Unless . . ."

Angela waited. It was obvious that Chrissy needed to be coaxed. "Unless what?"

"Well," Chrissy said, "I've been thinking a lot about Miss Dixon. You know, how she said she saw the ghost of John Ambrose Blue. Naturally, no one believed her."

"Naturally," Angela agreed.

"I have two classes with her. Music Theory and Introduction to Opera. I've gotten to know her pretty well. Sometimes I go to her apartment at night and we listen to records or watch an opera on television."

"What is the point you're making?" Angela asked.

"She's not a crazy person. People make fun of her because she's old, she's never been married, she likes to wear a lot of jewelry, and she dresses in long skirts. She's different, I'll say that, but she's far from crazy. If I were on a deserted island and had my choice of one person to be stranded with—out of everyone I know—I'd pick Miss Dixon. You know why? Because she'd find a way to get us home."

Angela was finding it difficult to see the point. "What are you telling me?"

"I'm saying that if she said she saw his ghost—she saw his ghost."

Angela stared at her friend. "The ghost of John Ambrose Blue is behind all these things?"

"Has to be," Chrissy said flatly.

"There are no such thing as ghosts," Angela said, just as matter-of-factly.

"Sorry," the librarian said. "You'll have to leave. It's closing time."

The girls quickly gathered the books and deposited them on the return desk.

Angela and Chrissy walked silently back to the cottage.

"You mad at me?" Chrissy finally asked.

"No." Angela smiled. "Maybe you're right about the whole thing."

"The ghost?"

"No. I don't buy that. I think your friend had a few drinks after dinner and she saw something all right, but not a ghost. Maybe all the things that have happened around here have been a coincidence. As of this moment, I am out of the detective business."

The girls linked arms and walked toward the cottage, the conversation centered around the costume party.

"See you at the dance," Chrissy said as she headed toward her room.

Angela managed a weak smile. She wasn't looking forward to wearing a diaper.

An orange jack-o'-lantern, with a single jagged tooth, grinned at the students as they entered the gym, which was decked out with black and orange streamers. A witch in a black pointed hat led them to their tables, where a vampire took their food orders. Señor Flores, wearing a dark shirt and tights beneath a flaming red cape, strutted about the dance floor with his wife.

"Guess he couldn't convince her to dress like a bull," Chrissy giggled.

She and Angela were concealed behind the kitchen door, peeking through the small glass window. They watched as the crowd suddenly burst into applause at two new arrivals.

Mr. Shulte, dressed in a white suit and straw hat, entered with Milli, who was costumed in a billowing gown à la Scarlett O'Hara.

"She looks like she's feeling fine," Angela exclaimed. "Glad the faculty isn't eligible for prizes. I'd be dead."

Headmaster Norseworthy paraded about in his baseball uniform, while his wife looked decidedly silly as a football player.

Chrissy pointed. "Do you believe that!"

Angela gaped at the sight of Mrs. Rome, in orange hair, sporting a body-hugging leather pantsuit with snakeskin boots.

"What is she supposed to be?" Chrissy asked.

"A punk rocker, I guess."

They noted that Mr. Rome was not present.

"He's probably embarrassed to be seen with her," Chrissy observed.

"I know the feeling. I'm embarrassed to be seen with me," Angela said, tugging at the white tablecloth pinned around her body. Her feet were wrapped in white woolen booties, made for her by Mrs. Neely.

"I feel like a jerk."

Chrissy reached over and straightened

the lace bonnet tied over Angela's long dark hair. "You do look adorable."

"Adorable! She looks fantastic!" Kevin boomed, as he entered the kitchen wheeling a huge steel shopping cart.

"Where did you steal that from?" Angela asked.

"I borrowed it from the supermarket. They know about it, so don't worry."

Angela stared at the white blanket and pillow tucked neatly around the cart.

"You expect me to get into that?"

He smiled. "Think of the fifty dollars," he said.

"Why did I ever let you talk me into such a stupid thing?"

"Because you're secretly crazy about me," he said, helping her into the cart.

"Don't forget this," Chrissy said, taking the baby bottle from her purse.

"I have a feeling I will never forget this as long as I live," Angela said mournfully.

"How do I look?" Kevin asked, turning around to show off the sharp creases in his spanking white navy uniform.

"Great," Angela said, "but you're missing one thing."

"What?"

"This," Chrissy said, handing him a three-pound can of spinach.

"I don't really have to eat it, do I?" he

asked. "That stuff makes me sick. I don't even like looking at it."

"If we lose—I'll shove it down your throat," Angela told him.

"And I'll help her," Chrissy said, adjusting the wings to her bumblebee costume.

"Just what I need—pressure!"

"Think of the fifty dollars," Angela said, smiling sweetly.

"Ready?" he asked, positioning himself behind the cart.

Angela moaned. "I'll never be ready for this. Let's just do it and get it over with."

They were just about to push through the doors when a roar of applause filled the room. The trio looked through the window and watched as Selena and April made their grand entrance. Selena, decked out in gold shorts and a gold blouse, clutched a gleaming sword next to her hip. April, clothed in green, flitted about her in Peter Pan boots.

"We don't have a chance," Angela said.

Kevin grinned. "We're just going to have to try harder."

"How?"

"Like this," he said, sticking the baby bottle in her mouth.

Before she could protest, Chrissy threw open the doors and Kevin wheeled her out into the gym singing at the top of his lungs, "I'm Popeye the sailorman . . ."

Eight

The next day, her share of the winning prize tucked snugly in her dungaree pocket, Angela sat with Chrissy in the back of Carmela's station wagon as they headed for three carefree days in the city.

It was the first visit home since entering Glencora, and Angela looked forward to introducing Chrissy to her neighborhood friends.

Chrissy's parents, who lived in Vermont, had called Jed Hart and given their approval for the visit.

"I want to see the Statue of Liberty, Radio City, Chinatown, the World Trade Center, the Bronx zoo, and the U.N.," Chrissy said excitedly.

Angela gave her a "get serious" look. "All I want to do is eat and sleep," she said.

"That's boring."

"So are all those places you mentioned."

"I'll risk it," Chrissy said.

"The first place we're going," Carmela said, "is to Engine Company 44. Dixie's taking us to lunch."

Angela liked him the moment she saw him striding toward the car. "Okay, ladies," he announced, sliding behind the steering wheel. "I'm not on duty till midnight, so where do we want to go?"

From there it was a blur of events. They lunched on a riverboat docked on the Hudson River. Then they visited the Central Park zoo and took pictures of the seals at feeding time. Then it was off to the observation deck of the Empire State Building, a quick stop at St. Patrick's Cathedral, dinner in Chinatown, and finally home, where a weary Angela and Chrissy collapsed into bed.

The next day, shortly before noon, Chrissy woke with a start, listening to loud crashing and banging.

"What's that?" she asked, shaking Angela awake.

"That's only Mikey," Angela mumbled.

"Is he mad at someone?"

"He's cooking lunch. Go back to sleep."

The next two days flew by, and soon they were back in the car, with bundles of clean laundry and food supplies, heading back to their mountaintop.

Chrissy sat in the back seat writing a letter to her mother. Angela had been silent most of the trip, her head buried in a spiral notebook.

"I told her it was the best vacation I ever had," Chrissy said, sealing the letter. "What are you writing?"

"Nothing," Angela said, suddenly closing the book.

"You've been at it for two days. What is it?"

"Nothing. Just writing down things," Angela said, tossing the book aside.

"Well, if you want to keep it a secret," Chrissy said, sounding injured.

"I just don't think you'd be interested."

"Try me," Chrissy challenged.

Angela reluctantly picked up the book and placed it open on her lap.

She turned to a page headed MOTIVES. Underneath she had listed:

Greed
Jealousy
Revenge

Ambition
Fear
Money
Insanity

The facing page was headed SUSPECTS. The page was blank.

Another page revealed THE POEM with certain words and phrases underlined: *A kingly visit, her, fourscore, a stranger.*

Under the heading MYSTERIOUS EVENTS she had noted

Records stolen from infirmary.
Mr. Shulte poisoned.
Mrs. Portnoy sees ghost.
Chandelier falls.
Figure by the graveyard.
Miss Dixon sees ghost.
"The end is near" written on wall.
Milli is injured.

One page was divided into two sections:

WHO WILL BENEFIT FROM SCHOOL'S DESTRUCTION?
 Students.
WHO WILL SUFFER?
 Teachers, staff, all employees.

The final page was headed WHAT TO DO NEXT. Three items were listed:

1. *Check old school yearbooks for back-ground on school and teachers.*
2. *Read John Ambrose Blue's novels for any possible clues.*
3. *Find out who's buried in graveyard.*

"That's all I have so far," Angela said, closing the book.

"It's not much. In fact, it's very little," Chrissy pointed out. "Besides," she added, "I thought you retired from the detective business."

"I did."

"Then . . . ?"

Angela placed the notebook on her lap and stared at the blank pages. She closed the book and confronted her friend.

"If I'm going to the store and I see you as I'm going across the street, that's a coincidence. If I come out of the store and you're standing down the block, that could also be a coincidence. If I go to the movies that night and you come in and sit a row away—that's planned."

Chrissy took the book and opened it to the page marked SUSPECTS. She stared at the empty page for a long time and then reached into her school bag and drew out a pencil. She scribbled, "The ghost of John Ambrose Blue," and handed the notebook back to Angela.

"That's fine," Angela agreed. "We have a suspect. That's more than we had before. So we'll pursue it and see what we come up with."

The girls were silent for the rest of the ride.

Milli was raking leaves into lumpy mounds in front of the cottage when Angela and Chrissy returned.

"How was the city?" Milli asked.

"Great!" Chrissy said, lugging her laundry bag up the steps. "See you at dinner," she told Angela and disappeared into the dorm.

"How are you feeling?" Angela asked the teacher.

"Just fine. Turned out to be just a bump." She smiled. "Your mom pack me any tidbits from the restaurant?"

"Yep. She even threw in some bones for Ruffles."

A guarded look crossed Milli's face.

"What's wrong?" Angela asked.

"Ruffles almost died. He was very sick."

"What happened?"

"The vet thinks he picked up some poison mushrooms in the woods. Mr. Lang found him down by the tennis courts."

Angela found the news disturbing. "I never saw any mushrooms in the woods."

"Me neither," Milli said.

Angela was about to blurt out that maybe someone poisoned him, but her words were cut off by Kevin, who shouted her name as he ran up the small hill.

She felt herself smiling.

"Come on," he said, taking her hand and yanking her off the porch.

"But—my clothes!"

Milli said, "Go ahead. I'll carry them in."

Within moments Angela was racing across the field.

"Where are we going?" she yelled through strands of hair plastered against her face by the wind.

"Home," he said, pulling her faster.

They reached his house and leapt over the porch steps. He led her through the door, across the foyer, and up the staircase to his room. Mr. and Mrs. Neely, who sat in the living room watching television, smiled as the two figures whizzed past.

Kevin threw open the door to his room, which was cluttered with athletic trophies, sports equipment, and baseball pennants. Angela collapsed on the edge of the bed, panting for breath.

"This better be good," she warned him.

Kevin laughed. "Now I know why I

missed you this weekend. You're such a cynic."

It suddenly occurred to Angela that she had never been in a boy's room before.

"Look at these," he said, proudly extending a stack of photographs.

She gazed down at the crisp black and white photos, which still smelled of some chemical compound.

"You took these with your new camera?"

"Yep. And I developed them in the school lab just an hour ago. I have another batch to do tonight."

Angela looked down at the image of Mr. Rome, bunched up in his jacket, sitting under a tree smoking a cigarette.

"See how I caught the cigarette smoke curling up in the air?" Kevin pointed out.

He also "caught" Mrs. Rome washing her car, Mrs. Portnoy at the mailbox, Headmaster Norseworthy talking to a student, and Mr. Shulte and Milli in deep conversation outside the cottage.

"You really made a pest of yourself, didn't you?" Angela teased.

"Come on," he said, and led her back down the stairs and out the house and across to Spy Rock—a huge boulder that protruded from the ground near the recreation hall.

"Is this trip necessary?" she moaned, shivering in the brisk air.

"If you're going to be my model, you better get used to this," he said, circling her and clicking away.

Angela never enjoyed having her picture taken under the best of circumstances, and her wooden poses revealed her dislike.

"Loosen up. Pretend you're having fun! Think of chocolate sundaes and pizza," Kevin barked.

Angela laughed despite her mood and was rewarded by an enthusiastic "Great! Fabulous! Keep that look."

Twenty-four clicks later, Kevin covered the lens with a plastic chip.

"I'll stop by after dinner and show them to you. Have to go. Basketball practice," he said, giving her a quick kiss on the cheek before dashing off.

Angela found his energy exhausting but, she had to admit, also exciting. She walked slowly toward her cottage, enjoying the autumn scent of pine cones in the air. Across the field, behind her cottage, she could see a single curl of smoke, much like the one in the photograph coming from the cigarette.

Her first thought was that Milli was burning leaves, but then the smoke thickened and yellow flames shot through the air.

Angela ran toward the cottage as girls spilled from the dorm and grouped on the lawn yelling and waving their arms.

She ran faster and saw the roof ignite into an orange balloon.

She stopped a few yards away as her face was stung by the intense heat. In the distance, fire engine sirens could be heard lumbering up the mountain. She knew the cottage would be gone before they arrived.

She also knew, without knowing why, that the fire probably started in her room.

Nine

A grim-faced headmaster toured the ruins of the cottage the following morning, accompanied by Jed Hart and the fire chief. Now and then a gust of wind would riffle through the gray, powdery cinders, sending dust and ashes dancing through the air. Only the tall, stately flagstone fireplace stood erect amid the destruction. All the rooms and walls had collapsed around it.

Chrissy and Angela stood behind a large table a few yards away, dispensing coffee to the workers who had spent all night clearing away the debris.

"We can be thankful that no one was

hurt," the fire chief said, accepting a cup of coffee from Angela.

Norseworthy forced a smile. "Yes. We were very lucky."

With classes suspended for the day, some students sat on the grass, watching. Others trudged past carrying linens and clothing to the gym, which temporarily housed the girls evicted by the fire.

Standing aside, away from the army of workers, Headmaster Norseworthy listened intently as the fire chief consulted his notes and said, "There's little doubt that the fire started in the front, first floor, room six."

He visibly winced as he realized the room belonged to Angela and April, two of his favorite students. He recalled unhappily that Angela had been previously chastised for smoking in the room—although she had denied the incident.

"Any idea how it started?"

"We've ruled out electrical combustion. As far as we can determine by the manner in which the structure ignited and the intensity of the fire, the cause was most likely careless error."

"Can you be more specific?"

"I'd say a cigarette was thrown in a waste basket."

Norseworthy felt his stomach tighten. "That will be your official report?"

"I'm afraid so."

Norseworthy thanked the man for his help and marched directly to his office, signaling Jed Hart to follow. "I want to see Angela, April, and Miss Greene in my office immediately," the headmaster ordered.

"I'll take care of it right away."

Ten

"I don't think he believed me," Angela told Chrissy. The girls were in the basement of the Neely house setting up army cots in their new living quarters. "Even Milli told him that I never went in the room, that she had carried my stuff in. But I know he didn't believe us. It's because of that time Selena was smoking and left her cigarette in the room and the monitor came in and reported me smoking."

"You think April did it?" Chrissy asked.

"She would no more touch a cigarette than she would a candy bar. You know what a health nut she is," Angela said.

"What did Milli say?"

"She said she unlocked the room, put my stuff on the bed, and then went back outside to finish raking the leaves. She left the door open because she figured I'd be right back. Anyone could've gone in there."

"Did she see anyone?"

"Everyone was there. Miss Dixon, Mrs. Rome. Even Mr. Lang stopped by to give Selena her science book. Señor Flores was there stacking up firewood by the fireplace."

"And I saw Jed Hart," Chrissy told her. "He was tacking up notices on the bulletin board."

"Any one of them could have done it," Angela said.

"No one did anything. It was an accident," Chrissy said firmly.

"Sure, just like all the others," Angela said just as firmly.

Mrs. Neely came into the room with a lamp that Kevin had retrieved from the attic. "We'll turn this into a real pretty room," she said with a smile.

"It was very nice of you to let us stay here," Chrissy said, placing her clothes in the bureau drawers.

"We're happy to have you," Mrs. Neely said, adjusting the freshly starched window curtains. "I'm just sorry we don't have enough room to take in some of the other girls. The attic is much too drafty."

Angela was secretly glad that April had opted to move in with Mr. and Mrs. Rome, who also agreed to house Selena. Chrissy had been invited to share a bedroom with Nurse Samuels but had jumped at the opportunity to room with Angela in the Neely basement.

While they were unpacking, Kevin arrived.

"You'll never guess what happened," he said, plopping himself on the cot.

"The navy saw you in the Popeye costume and drafted you," Angela replied.

"I got a job. A real job! Yesterday, when all the reporters were here I talked to Mr. Eagleton, the editor of *The Glenwell Gazette*. I showed him my pictures. He thought they were very good, and he hired me to cover our sports. He's going to pay me for every picture and story he uses."

"That's great," Angela said.

"If it wasn't for you, none of this would have happened. When I get my first paycheck, I'm taking you to dinner in town."

"What about me?" Chrissy chimed in. "She wasn't going to wear that diaper, but I talked her into doing it."

"Dinner for three! When they see how good I am, they'll probably give me an expense account. Oh, almost forgot," he said, reaching into his jacket pocket. He handed Angela a stack of photos.

"What's this?"

"The pictures I took of you the other day."

Angela and Chrissy shuffled through the photos. "Not bad," Angela had to admit. He had taken various poses of her sitting, standing, and stretched out on Spy Rock.

"Pretty sexy," Chrissy said, eyeing a photo of Angela standing on the rock with her hair blowing across her face and her hands on her hips.

"I'm thinking of blowing that one up," Kevin grinned. "That's my favorite."

Angela glanced at the black and white photo and suddenly her heart quickened. "What's that?" she asked, pointing. The cottage was visible in the background surrounded by a slight fog covering. But it wasn't fog, it was smoke.

"Isn't that something! I noticed that. The fire must have just started when I took that picture."

Angela quickly skimmed the other photos and stopped when she spotted a blurred figure, rounding the corner of the cottage.

"Who's that?" Angela asked, hoping her voice sounded casual.

"I never noticed that before," Kevin said,

squinting at the photo. "Wouldn't you know it! Somebody got in the way."

Angela stared at the blurred figure of a man. He was coming from behind the cottage just moments after the fire had started. Though distant and slightly out of focus, there was no mistaking the familiar slump of the body.

"It's Mr. Theopopolis," Chrissy said matter-of-factly.

"Well, I gotta go," Kevin said, taking the photos. "I'll make you up a set of prints. I'll bring my TV down later so you can watch it. I won't have time with my new job." He dashed for the door and paused to say "Glad you're staying with us" before running out.

"Imagine! A TV in our room!" Chrissy said. "Boy, I'm gonna love it here."

Angela sat silently for a few moments. "You never mentioned that Mr. Theopopolis was by the cottage the day of the fire."

"Of course not. I didn't see him."

"Neither did Milli. That's strange. She listed every person she saw. I was there when she told Norseworthy—but she never mentioned Mr. Theopopolis."

"She probably didn't see him either. What's the big deal?"

"I'm not sure!"

"Oh, I get it," Chrissy said, somewhat annoyed. "Another listing for your notebook! When are you going to give up?"

Angela froze.

The look on her face frightened her roommate.

"What's wrong?"

"The notebook!" Angela gasped. "I had forgotten all about it!"

"So?"

Angela felt the words forming in her mind but was scared to allow them to come out.

"You're making me nervous," Chrissy said. "What's going on?"

"Someone saw the notebook! Milli said she threw my stuff on the bed. The notebook was right on top of the laundry bag. Not inside of it. On top. It was probably right there on the bed, and while I was with Kevin someone went in the room and read the notebook. That's why he burned the room!"

Chrissy gasped. "You're crazy. That's the weirdest thing I ever heard. Who would burn a room just because . . ."

"Because that person knows I'm getting closer. Maybe something in my notes hit on something. I was getting close, that much he knew. So he had to destroy the evidence."

"But all he had to do was steal it! He didn't

have to burn down the room!" Chrissy protested.

"And risk getting caught with it later. Maybe he didn't have time to hide it. He heard someone coming. So he set it on fire and threw it in the wastebasket."

Chrissy, despite her earlier confidence, was finding herself being drawn into the theory. Something about it, as crazy as it sounded, was starting to make sense in a terrifying way.

"If that's true, then the person who did it knows you're on to something."

"Exactly." Angela was trembling. "That means," she said in a shaking voice, "sooner or later he has to make a move against me."

Eleven

At dinner that evening Angela found herself seated with four seniors, Mr. Slavin, Señor Flores, and Miss Dixon.

Chrissy, who was on kitchen detail, was busy filling water glasses and taking food orders.

"Tell me, Angela," Mr. Slavin said, munching on his salad, "have you made a dent in the reading list I handed out last week?"

"No, sir," she mumbled.

"May I ask why?"

"Well, actually, I did start a book, but it wasn't on your list."

"Some light entertainment, I assume?"

"A biography of John Ambrose Blue."

Mr. Flores laughed. "Hardly light reading. Personally, I consider him a very minor talent."

"There are those that would disagree," Mr. Slavin observed. "I, for one," he added.

"I was just curious about him," Angela said, sipping her tea. "Especially since I learned about the poem."

"That particular piece is a very poor effort," Miss Dixon chimed in. "If one of my students had turned in such a paper he would've received a very unsatisfactory grade."

Angela plunged forward. "But what about his predictions?" she asked, her eyes darting quickly between the three teachers, hoping to catch a glimmer of reaction. "They say there are people who can predict the future."

"And some primitive cultures believe that a broken mirror condemns one to seven years of misfortune," Miss Dixon said.

"Nonetheless," Mr. Slavin said, putting down his fork, "some very strange things are happening on this campus."

"We're just going through an unfortunate phase," Miss Dixon said. "It happens to individuals, businesses, nations. Nothing is immune from an occasional unlucky streak."

"I suppose," Slavin said, but he didn't

sound totally convinced. "Speaking of bad luck, did you hear about Mr. Theopopolis?"

Miss Dixon nodded grimly. "Yes. I felt very bad."

"What? What?" Angela asked excitedly, trying not to scream.

"I'm afraid I'm in the dark," Señor Flores told them.

"He's been fired," Miss Dixon whispered.

"No! When?"

"He received the news this afternoon," she said. "He was told his contract would not be renewed at the end of the year."

"Everyone knew it was coming. I knew it a year ago," Mr. Slavin said. "It was only a matter of time."

"Why?" Angela blurted out before she could stop herself.

"He and the headmaster don't exactly see eye to eye," Miss Dixon said, cutting her food into neat little pieces. Chrissy was right, Angela observed. She's very controlled.

"By all rights he should have been headmaster," Mr. Slavin said. "I guess he never forgave the school for appointing someone off the campus."

"Can't say I blame him," Señor Flores said. "Certainly no one has been here longer. Why, Mr. Theopopolis was actually born here on the mountain when his parents were teachers here."

"That may be," Miss Dixon added, "but I think the school made an excellent choice in Mr. Norseworthy. He was a very successful university administrator in Georgia. He came with the highest credentials. We're lucky to have him."

"That's a matter of opinion," one of the seniors said, which caused the other boys to burst out laughing.

The laughter was abruptly cut off by the sudden appearance of Jed Hart. He approached the table and spoke directly to Angela.

"Mr. Norseworthy would like you to attend a meeting at his house immediately after dinner."

A half hour later Mrs. Norseworthy greeted Angela at the door and invited her to join the others in the study. As she hurried along the carpeted foyer with its antique furnishings, she was happy to spot Ruffles napping near the kitchen stove.

"Come in, Angela," the headmaster said, rising from behind his large mahogany desk. "Make yourself comfortable."

Angela chose a floor cushion next to Milli and Chrissy. She noted that Kevin was in the room. Seated on the couch, on chairs, and on the window seat were April, Selena, Mr.

Theopopolis, Mr. Shulte, Mrs. Portnoy, Mr. Lang, Mr. Neely, and Mr. Rome. Other students from the dorm were also in attendance.

"The reason I've invited all of you," the headmaster said, "is to discuss the recent fire. I've already spoken with Mr. Slavin, Señor Flores, and Miss Dixon, so I saw no need to include them tonight. Nurse Samuels and Mr. Hart have also been excused, as they have duties to attend to."

The elderly Theopopolis spoke out. "Perhaps you can dispense with me also, as I have papers to grade." The tone of his voice made it sound like a demand rather than a request. It did not go undetected by the headmaster.

Norseworthy confronted him. "You were seen near the cottage at the time of the fire."

The old man glared. "Was I?"

"Yes."

Angela spun to look at Kevin, who avoided her inquiring eyes. Why did you show him the picture? she wanted to shout.

"Can you explain your being there?"

"I was walking in the woods when I heard a commotion. Students were running. I could see the smoke and knew there was a fire. When I was satisfied that everyone had been evacuated, I went home."

"You didn't wait for the firemen?"

"Why should I? I'm not trained to put out fires."

Mr. Norseworthy showed his dissatisfaction with the reply.

"Weren't you even curious?"

"I'm not given to curiosity."

"Tell me, do you walk in the woods often?"

"Quite often." Angela felt rather than heard the old man's rage.

"Did you see anyone lurking about the cottage prior to the fire?"

"No."

Mr. Norseworthy hesitated a moment. "Would you tell me if you had?"

"Probably not."

The headmaster made a note and dismissed the history teacher. The old man gathered up his books and hastily retreated.

For the next two hours the headmaster questioned the others and jotted down their responses. It was all Angela could do to keep awake. She forced herself to focus her attention on a single item, to keep her eyes open. The object was the gold tie clip across the headmaster's chest with the chunky initials *HN*.

None of the information offered had been earth-shattering:

Mr. Neely had been there to measure the

window frames for the winter installation of storm windows.

Selena had entered April and Angela's room to borrow glue from April, and finding the room empty, had left.

Mrs. Portnoy told of visiting one of her students to tutor her for a test.

Jed Hart had tacked up his notice on the bulletin board and left, stopping briefly to chat with Milli, who had been raking leaves.

Mr. Rome had seen Mr. Flores stacking the firewood as he sat in the parlor area.

Bob Shulte said he had gone to Milli's room to surprise her with a box of candy. Getting no response, he had opened the door and entered. He paused to write a note and left it, along with the candy, on her desk. He hadn't seen her upon entering or leaving the cottage.

"How is that possible if she was outside raking leaves?" Norseworthy asked.

"Easy. I always use the back entrance. It's a more direct route from my cottage."

The headmaster finally thanked everyone for their cooperation and invited anyone who wished to speak to him privately to call his office in the morning.

Chrissy, Angela, and Kevin walked from the house together. "Why did you tell him about the picture?" Angela asked.

"I didn't," Kevin said. "I showed it to Mr.

Rome, and he must have told Norseworthy that Theopopolis was in the vicinity. I'm not crazy about the old coot, but I wouldn't try to get him in trouble."

"Does Mr. Rome have a grudge against him?"

"Face it. Nobody likes him. Except maybe Miss Dixon. It's his own fault. He's grouchy," Kevin said.

"Have you ever heard of Mrs. Portnoy going to a student's room to tutor her?" Chrissy asked.

"Never," Angela said. "She always says if you're not prepared, you fail."

"I think Norseworthy is making too much of this," Kevin said. "Someone ditched a cigarette and the place burned down. He's never going to get the person to admit it."

Later that night, lying on cots comfortably padded with double quilts, Angela and Chrissy listened to Mrs. Neely's footsteps overhead.

"Guess we'll have to get used to that," Chrissy said, glancing up from the romance novel she was reading.

Angela smiled and said, "Somehow I can't imagine Mr. Shulte bringing candy. He doesn't seem the romantic type."

Chrissy yawned. "If he was, he won't be anymore."

"What do you mean?"

"When I was serving dinner tonight, Miss Greene and Mr. Shulte were having what you could call a fight. Not loud or anything, but he was very annoyed."

"Really? Do you know what it was about?"

"He wanted her to go to his family's for Thanksgiving break and she didn't want any part of it."

"They'll probably patch it up," Angela said. "It's obvious they're crazy about each other."

Angela filled her in about Mr. Theopopolis being fired.

"Where will he go?" Chrissy said.

"Who knows? But," Angela said slowly, "if you had been born here and lived all your life on this mountain and suddenly they want to get rid of you . . ."

"Forget it," Chrissy said. She started to say something else, but her attention was drawn to a figure by the window that crouched on its hands and knees to peer into the basement room.

Chrissy screamed and Angela turned just in time to see a blue cape swirl away into the night.

"It's him! It's him!" Chrissy yelled. Angela rushed to her side just as Mrs. Neely ran into the room.

"What's wrong? What happened?"

"Nothing," Angela said quickly. "Chrissy just had a nightmare. Everything's okay."

Mrs. Neely said she understood and invited them upstairs for a snack.

"Maybe later," Angela said. "Thanks." She waited till she heard Mrs. Neely's footsteps on the stairs.

"You okay?" she asked Chrissy.

The frightened girl nodded. "Did you see him?"

"I saw something. I'm not sure what."

"He was wearing the cape," Chrissy cried. "He's come back from the dead and he's going to get us all."

Angela reached for her jacket and headed for the door.

"Where are you going? You can't leave me alone," Chrissy pleaded.

"I'll be right back," Angela said.

Chrissy jumped and took her jacket from the door hook. "You're not leaving me here alone," she said, following her friend.

Angela walked slowly up the stairs that led to the kitchen and was relieved to find that Mrs. Neely was nowhere to be seen.

"What are you doing?" Chrissy asked as Angela opened the cabinet under the sink. She watched while Angela searched through the jumble of cleaning detergents, soaps, and assorted tools.

"Great!" Angela said, bringing out a flashlight. "Come on!"

"Where are we going?" Chrissy said, following meekly.

"Just outside."

Within moments they were standing by the window looking into their bedroom.

"Let's get out of here. He might come back," Chrissy warned. Not even a sliver of the moon penetrated the thick darkness of the mountaintop. Across the road the familiar howling of wild dogs filled the night.

Angela directed the yellow beacon of the flashlight to the ground.

"Look," she told Chrissy.

"What?"

"Footprints," Angela said, shining the light on a soft piece of ground that had recently been dug up to protect the flower beds against winter.

"That proves I saw him!" Chrissy said.

"It proves something else," Angela said grimly.

"What?"

"Ghosts don't leave footprints."

Twelve

The next day, after class, Chrissy and Angela
were back in the school library and settled
in for a long stint at a corner table.

It had been Chrissy's idea. She was now
determined to unravel the mystery of the
poem.

As Angela pored through aged yearbooks,
school brochures, and newspaper clippings,
Chrissy constructed a large diagram showing the name of every person on the mountain, with lines drawn between the names of
people who had any special connection with
each other.

"A direct line is the shortest distance between two points," Chrissy said. "When our

project is finished, one of those lines is going to point to the person behind all this."

Angela wasn't so sure. She would have preferred to mount a scouting party to try to find the blue cape hidden in someone's closet, but she was so grateful to have Chrissy finally on her side that she didn't want to dampen her enthusiasm.

"Did you know that Miss Dixon and Mrs. Rome once wrote a cookbook together and even appeared on a local TV show?" Angela asked, refolding the yellowed clipping.

"Nope."

"Yeah, it was a barbecue cookbook. Interesting. I didn't even know they liked each other," Angela said.

She watched as Chrissy drew a red magic marker line between the two women's names. Chrissy then went back to the yearbooks.

"Here's something interesting," she said as she slid the page over to Angela. "Did you know that Milli was a student of Mr. Norseworthy's when they were both at the university in Georgia?"

"She mentioned something about being from the South, but I never paid any attention. I mean, everyone is from somewhere."

Chrissy continued reading. "It seems they were friends, and she joined the staff two years after he became headmaster.

"Makes sense," Angela said. "If I could help a friend find a job, I would."

Chrissy agreed, but drew the red line between the two names nonetheless.

"How are Sherlock and Watson doing?" a voice interrupted.

They looked up in time to see Kevin pull up a chair. "Any clues yet?"

"None," Angela confessed. She had finally taken him into her confidence and had spilled the whole story. To his credit, he had not scoffed at the girls' theory.

"I've been thinking about what you told me. I can't say I buy it one hundred percent, but I also don't want to discourage you—just in case it's true. So," he said, reaching into his football jacket and producing a crumpled piece of paper, "during history I jotted down some things about our mountain dwellers. It may not amount to anything, but . . . there it is. However, you're not to tell anyone where you heard this."

Chrissy and Angela both lunged for the paper, but Chrissy had the faster hand. Her eyes darted about the scribbled notes quickly.

"Wow! This is hot stuff! You sure about this?"

"Most of it is common knowledge. You forget, I've lived here a long time."

Chrissy continued reading and flipped the paper over. "Wow!"

"Can I get in on it?" Angela asked.

Chrissy unfolded the wrinkles of the paper and laid it flat on the desk.

"Mr. Rome was fired for drinking with one of the students but he got his job back when Mrs. Rome told them she was going to have a baby and they needed the job."

"I didn't know they had kids," Angela said.

"They don't," Kevin answered. "She lost the baby. She and Señora Flores had been ice-skating one night on the pond by the tennis courts and Mrs. Rome fell."

Angela watched as Chrissy drew a line between Señora Flores and Mrs. Rome. There was another line going from Mr. Rome's name to a box marked THE SCHOOL.

Angela picked up the paper and read Kevin's notes. " 'Nurse Samuels was engaged to a teacher, but he was fired for borrowing the school van and cracking it up. He left school the next day without a word to anyone, and Nurse Samuels continued to defend him, saying the punishment had been too harsh.' This stuff is terrific!

" 'Mr. Shulte punched Mr. Lang in the face, and even though the police came, no charges were pressed.' "

"What was that about?" Chrissy asked.

"I'm not sure. It was a couple of years ago. They never got along. Still don't."

"What's this note here?" Angela said, squinting.

Kevin took the paper. "Oh, that. I wasn't even going to put it down, but you told me to include everything. About two years ago Mrs. Norseworthy left her husband and went back to Georgia to live. She returned after a few weeks, and no one ever mentioned it. But for a while everyone thought they'd get a divorce."

"Any reason why she left?"

"My mother said at the time that Norseworthy probably had a girlfriend and his wife found out, but that's ridiculous. Anyone who knows him knows that can't be the reason."

"Maybe he's a gambler. Or a drinker," Chrissy said.

Angela found it hard to believe any of the theories. He just wasn't the type.

"Maybe Mrs. Norseworthy had a boyfriend and she left to be with him and it didn't work out," Angela said, finding that equally hard to believe.

"Just put a question mark next to their names," Kevin suggested. "I don't have the answer and I'm not about to ask them."

Angela continued to the next item on the

list: "Mr. Theopopolis and Mrs. Portnoy were missing for twenty-four hours."

"You're kidding!"

"No. One day neither of them showed for class, they weren't at dinner, and the next morning they showed up in a cab and never explained where they were or what had happened."

"And Norseworthy let him get away with it?"

"That was when Mr. Hilly was headmaster, and he was a very close friend of Mr. Theopopolis. But after Mr. Hilly died, a lot of people still remembered that incident. Some people think that's the reason the trustees didn't appoint Theopopolis headmaster and picked Norseworthy instead."

Chrissy drew another red line, this time between the history teacher and Mrs. Portnoy. "I'm gonna run out of red," she laughed. "This stuff is better than my soap operas."

"Anything else?" Angela asked.

"Just this," Kevin said. "I heard a few weeks ago that Nurse Samuels's boyfriend was seen hanging around town."

"Are you positive? Who told you?" Angela asked.

"My father. He had taken the truck in to be overhauled and was sitting in the bar waiting for the work to be done when he walked in. My father bought him a beer."

"Does she know he's back?"

"My father didn't ask."

"Has your father seen him again?"

"He thought he spotted him the other day walking along the road when he was on his way to town for supplies. But he was driving too fast, so he couldn't be sure."

"Does this man have a name?" Chrissy asked.

"Danny."

Chrissy entered the name Danny and drew a line between it and THE SCHOOL.

"Would he know about the poem?" Angela asked.

Kevin looked at her for a long moment. "He taught English."

Angela felt her stomach jump.

"It was after he was fired that they hired Mr. Slavin," Kevin added.

The librarian flickered the lights to indicate she was closing the reading room.

Kevin jumped. "Look at the time! I have kitchen detail," he said, throwing on his jacket. "See you later."

Angela and Chrissy gathered up their papers, replaced the books on the shelf, and said good-night to the librarian. Angela noticed outside that she was still holding on to the scrap of paper that Kevin had given them.

"Do we need it?" she asked Chrissy.

"Naw, I have it all recorded on my graph," Chrissy said, clutching her note-book close.

Angela crumpled up the paper and threw it into a litter basket along the path.

They continued walking, oblivious to the figure that stood rigidly behind a tree.

They were laughing at the image of Mr. Shulte punching Mr. Lang in the nose, when, behind them, the dark figure reached quickly into the wire basket and retrieved the paper.

Thirteen

The long Thanksgiving weekend came and went, and for Angela the highlight had been spending time with her mother.

Chrissy had gone to Vermont to be with her family, and for the brief time away from Glencora, Angela had been able to push aside all thoughts of the strange campus happenings.

Sitting in a movie theater with her mom and Dixie, Angela noted that they held hands throughout the show. Glencora seemed like a long-forgotten novel.

On the long ride back to the mountain Angela had been momentarily tempted to tell her mother of the strange incidents, but she knew, realistically, how foolish it would sound to someone who had not experienced it.

It was ironic to Angela that now that she was adopting a "Maybe I'm the crazy one" attitude, Chrissy was poring over her charts and continuing the research. She had called from Vermont to say that John Ambrose Blue, in one of his published collections of short stories, had written a two-page dedication to his history teacher, Mr. Theopopolis's father.

"So? What's unusual about that? He obviously liked his teacher," Angela had replied. "That's hardly news."

Chrissy had paused. "The news is that the family died in a fire in the school."

"What!"

"The only ones that survived were the baby, our Mr. Theopopolis, and his father."

"You sure about this?"

"Positive. And then—here's the really strange thing—the father disappeared six months later and his body was never found."

"What do you mean disappeared?"

"He just vanished. Leaving the child behind."

Angela found the story disturbing.

"Are you saying now that it's the ghost of

Mr. Theopopolis's father who has come back to haunt the school?"

"I'm just saying that the old man is the key to this in some way."

They had finally hung up without resolving the new puzzle piece. For Angela the whole matter was growing too complex.

Back in their cozy basement room at the Neely house, the girls brought each other up to date on their vacations.

"My mother is definitely in love," Angela announced.

"How do you know?"

"She smiles all the time."

Chrissy agreed that the evidence was conclusive. She had noticed the same "affliction" whenever Angela and Kevin were together, but decided to keep it to herself.

After dinner the girls joined Kevin and his parents in the living room for a game of cards.

Kevin was hyped up, rattling on about the championship chess game that was going to take place on campus the following afternoon.

In an effort to raise funds to rebuild the cottage, a local businessman and Jed Hart had arranged for a chess tournament between Malcolm Tucker, the United States' ranking chess master and Lieutenant John Sykes, a noted contender from the Blazer

Military Academy. Proceeds from the sale of tickets and souvenir programs would go to the building fund. Mr. Eagleton had hired Kevin to photograph the event.

"He's paying me for the whole day, not just the pictures I take," Kevin said proudly, fingering the plastic press card clipped to his shirt pocket.

"Are you going to sleep with your badge?" Angela asked.

"Probably," Mrs. Neely said. "He hasn't taken it off since he got it."

"Besides that, anything exciting happen while we were gone?" Chrissy asked, ignoring Angela's kick to her shin under the table.

"Not that I can think of," Mr. Neely said, studying the cards in his hand.

"It was very quiet," his wife agreed, "except for poor Mr. Theopopolis."

Chrissy and Angela exchanged looks.

"What happened to him?"

"Hurt his leg," Mr. Neely said, drawing another card and placing it in his hand. "Told him he was a darn fool to be out there walking in the woods at night. Sure thing, he tripped over a hunter's trap. Lucky he has a leg left. Could've got himself really hurt bad."

"I took him his dinner tonight," Mrs. Neely said. "He's a strange one, all right."

Angela glanced at the clock on the kitchen wall and jumped up. "We have to go. Rehearsals started five minutes ago, and Mr. Shulte gets furious if anyone is late. Come on, Chrissy."

"Then hurry along," Mrs. Neely said. "We can't have our leading actresses thrown out of the show."

Angela grabbed up their jackets and waited while Chrissy caught up.

"Want me to walk you over?" Kevin offered.

"No thanks. We'll be okay."

Still, Angela thought, as they hurried out into the night, it had been nice of him to offer.

The campus was still, telling Angela that the other students had already arrived in the gym.

After four tryouts, Angela and Chrissy had landed the leading roles as the two elderly women in *Arsenic and Old Lace.* Selena and April had been chosen as costume and set designers.

As Angela and Chrissy approached the gym, they could hear angry voices on the other side of the door.

"It's probably Mr. Shulte yelling about us," Angela groaned. She hesitated to open the door.

The voices grew louder. It was Mr. Shulte

all right. "Let's discuss this. I think you owe me that much!" he was saying, his voice breaking.

"I'm sorry," someone replied.

"Sorry!" he thundered. "So that's it! That's your attitude? You're sorry!"

The door was thrown open, almost knocking Angela over, and they saw Milli rush past them, her eyes to the ground. Before they could react, she was out of earshot, rushing toward the recreation hall.

Angela and Chrissy timidly entered the gym in time to hear Mr. Shulte bark, "Everyone take your places!"

"Talk about a lovers' quarrel," Gary whispered as he took his place on the stage next to the girls.

"What happened?" Chrissy asked softly.

"We were waiting to start and Miss Greene walked in and they went to the back of the room and it looked like they were having a big argument." Gary shrugged.

Angela realized suddenly that since the fire she had seen very little of Milli. Gone were the nights of hot chocolate and cheese sandwiches. She decided she'd visit Milli soon in her new quarters, which she now shared with Señor and Señora Flores.

The rehearsals progressed smoothly and broke after two hours.

"Wanna stop in and visit Milli?" Angela

asked as she and Chrissy gathered their jackets.

"It's kind of late, isn't it?"

"We'll go by the cottage, and if the lights are on we'll ring the bell. What do you say?"

Chrissy thought it was dumb, but agreed to tag along. "She's probably not in the mood for visitors after her fight with Mr. Shulte."

"I think she'd be more than happy to see us," Angela persisted. "Anyway, it looks like she's home," she said, glancing toward the cottage. The lights from the Floreses' first-floor apartment shown brightly.

The girls rang the bell, which was answered by Señora Flores wearing a bathrobe.

"Is Miss Greene awake? We wanted to see her," Angela said.

"I'm sorry, she went out," the woman said. "But I'll tell her you were here."

"Okay, thanks," Angela said.

"She couldn't have gone too far," Angela told Chrissy as they walked from the cottage. "Her car was in the driveway."

"Boy, you don't miss anything, do you," Chrissy said, squinting in the darkness toward the bulky shape of the auto a few yards away.

"I just happened to notice it," Angela said.

"She's probably visiting someone on campus," Chrissy said.

An unexpected noise caused them to turn in the direction of the parked car. Although they were too far away to make out the figures, they could see two people walking away from the car.

Chrissy and Angela glanced at each other, but neither budged. They watched as one person climbed the porch steps; then, under the overhead light, they could see Milli entering the cottage. They watched as the other figure cut hurriedly across the campus. Both of them said the name at the same time.

"Mr. Norseworthy!"

The girls waited till he was out of view before resuming their walk home.

"What do you suppose that was all about?" Chrissy asked.

"She was probably upset about her argument and she wanted to tell the headmaster before he heard it from someone else."

"But why sit in a dark car?"

"She's probably still crying and doesn't want to be around a lot of people. I can understand that," Angela said.

"It just seems strange, that's all," Chrissy added.

Kevin was waiting for them on the porch when they arrived.

Angela broke into a grin. "Checking up to see what time we get home?"

His usual smile was missing.

"I have to show you something," he said, urging them to follow him.

"What is it?" Angela said as she and Chrissy hurried with him across the soccer field toward the recreation hall. Kevin reached the hall and held the door open. A few students sat at tables near the soda and candy machines, slouched over their books.

"Come on," Kevin said, leading the girls downstairs to the auditorium.

The huge room was bustling with activity as Mr. Lang, Señor Flores, and Miss Dixon scurried about the stage setting up folding chairs. Students sat at long tables stapling stacks of paper.

"What's going on?" Chrissy asked.

"They're getting ready for the chess match," Kevin said, mounting the stage and holding aside the backstage curtain for them.

Kevin led them down a narrow stairway to the basement under the stage. "I was here to help carry tables and chairs when Mr. Lang asked me to look in one of the boxes for some paint and brushes to make up a sign."

Angela found the place spooky. It was just

a large room with a light bulb dangling from the ceiling.

Kevin led them to a tiny alcove hidden beneath the stairway, where old newspapers and magazines were stacked in cartons next to a broken refrigerator and an old, tattered mattress.

"I was just hunting around and I looked in this box," Kevin said as he reached overhead and removed a small carton from a cement ledge.

"And?" Angela asked.

"I found this," Kevin said, opening the box and removing a blue cape.

Chrissy gasped. "That's . . . that's . . . !"

"Your ghost," Kevin said.

Fourteen

"Welcome to Glencora," the headmaster told the audience. "We're honored today to have such distinguished guests as Lieutenant Sykes and Mr. Tucker, and we thank all of you who have come out to witness this historic event. So . . . may the best man win."

Amid applause, the two men took their places at the table on the stage. A huge screen depicting the chess board hung from the wall, manned by Mr. Lang and Mrs. Portnoy, which would allow the audience to follow the chess game.

Chrissy and Angela, who had served as ushers, now stood in the rear of the hall.

Angela yawned loudly and Chrissy elbowed her.

"I'm sorry," Angela said, "but I find the whole thing extremely boring."

"Don't you realize that history is being made before our eyes?" Chrissy asked excitedly. Angela stifled another yawn and reached for one of the books she had brought along to catch up on her assignments.

"How can you read at a time like this?" Chrissy asked, not taking her eyes from the stage. "Look at Kevin."

Angela glanced up to see Kevin quietly stepping around the chess players as he clicked away from different angles. He moved swiftly and silently, almost like a ballet dancer, Angela noted with a degree of pride.

Chrissy gasped. "What a brilliant move! I never would have thought of that," she said.

Angela resumed reading.

"No wonder Tucker's the champ," Chrissy continued. "All he did was move his knight and now Sykes is in real trouble. I don't know what he's going to do."

Angela wished that Chrissy would keep from interrupting her studying.

"Now Sykes is moving *his* knight!" Chrissy said with amazement.

"Can't you see I'm trying to—" Angela

stopped in midsentence. She could feel her stomach churning. A pained expression crossed her face.

"What's wrong?" Chrissy asked.

Angela tried to hide the nervousness she was feeling. "What . . . what did you say before?"

"I don't know. Oh. I said he moved his knight."

Angela gripped Chrissy's arm.

"You're scaring me," Chrissy said, trying to move away from her friend's grasp.

"The poem!" Angela whispered, pulling Chrissy closer.

"What about it?"

"Don't you remember? He wrote about this!"

"He did?"

Angela stared ahead at the two men hunched over the chessboard and began quietly to recite:

"A kingly visit to herald the lights,
    A somber duel of silent knights."

Chrissy felt her heart flutter. "Are you sure?"

"Positive."

The two girls held on to each other, not saying a word, each lost in her own frightening thoughts.

* * *

Later that evening, lying in bed, Angela could not shake the fear that the poem's prophecy was racing ahead like an out-of-control train. It was only a matter of time before the collision.

She wished Chrissy was with her, but she had gone to Miss Dixon's room to listen to opera records. Kevin was at the newspaper office writing the story about the chess match and had called to say he'd be late.

Angela glanced at the bedside clock—it was almost nine o'clock. She could hear Mr. and Mrs. Neely talking overhead as they watched television. She gave up trying to fall asleep. She flung off the covers, dressed quickly, and quietly slipped out the side door.

The night air was unusually mild as she made her way quickly across the deserted campus. The wild dogs whined in the distance, but she knew from the sound that they were too far away to pose any danger.

Her fingers gripped the yellow plastic flashlight jammed in her pocket. Somehow, it gave her courage as she began the long descent down the mountainside to the gravestones.

Fearful of slipping, she edged her way slowly through the woods, clutching the tree barks as she stepped gingerly down the embankment. Her foot caught on a tree root, causing her to lose her balance, and she slid down the hill. A gust of wind bit at her fingertips.

Angela took out her flashlight and aimed it at the trees blocking her path. She recognized the rocky area and knew she was in the immediate area of the cemetery. She quickened her step. When she arrived at the spot where she and her mother had looked at the gravestones, she shone the light on the ground and stepped back in horror.

The graves had been dug up!

The headstones lay tossed aside and a large, gaping hole confronted her. She peered into the deep black pit and felt the ground sway. She felt herself falling and heard the flashlight strike a rock as it slid from her grasp. She was submerged in the warm darkness.

Angela awoke to find herself choking for air. The arid odor was overpowering, and she forced her lungs to expand. Almost instantly, the odor vanished.

"You'll be okay now," a voice assured her.

Angela glanced at the face peering down at her and jumped to her feet.

"It's all right, you're safe. Just take it easy."

Angela found herself staring at Mr. Theopopolis.

"That stuff smells terrible, but it did the trick," he smiled, showing her the bottle of household ammonia.

She looked around and discovered she was on the couch of the old man's apartment. Soft music filtered through the room crowded with antiques and silk lampshades with dangling tassles. It reminded her of a gypsy parlor she had visited on the boardwalk at Coney Island.

"Feeling better?"

"I think so." She smiled weakly. "How did I get here?"

"I carried you."

"Why didn't you take me to the Neely house?"

"I started to but then I realized we'd have to answer questions and I don't think we're ready to do that just yet," he said, massaging his swollen leg.

Angela had forgotten about his injury and wondered how he had managed to carry her that distance.

"You saved my life."

He shrugged. "You only fainted."

"But I could have fallen into the . . . hole." The image caused her to tremble. "What time is it?" she asked quickly.

"A little after ten," he said, glancing at the watch chained to his vest pocket.

"I better call the Neelys. If they check my room and find me gone, they'll get worried."

"Use the phone in the kitchen." He pointed. "And don't mention what happened. Tell them you're visiting a friend."

Angela nodded and hurried from the room.

Angela did as she was told. "Everything's fine. I told them I'd be another hour."

"Good."

She watched the old man as he poured two mugs of hot chocolate from the pitcher on a small table near his reading lamp. She accepted the drink gratefully.

Angela sat on the couch and faced the teacher. "What were you doing there when you found me?"

"Hiding," he said, blowing softly on the hot liquid in his cup.

"From whom?"

"I don't know. I've been hiding there for three nights. I have a feeling that whoever dug up the graves will be back. I want to find the person who did it. I was behind the tree when I heard you come down the hill. You made a lot of noise."

She smiled. "I tripped and slid down."

"When I saw it was you I started to announce myself, but then I was curious to find out what you were doing there. When you fainted, I grabbed you and carried you here. I was very careful. No one saw us."

"What do you mean?" There was a mysterious insinuation in his voice that alarmed her.

"I mean that the person who is out to make the poem come true doesn't know we're on to what is going on."

She suddenly felt a great sense of relief. "How did you know I've been trying to find the person?"

"Why else would you return to the graves?"

Angela exclaimed, "You were there the night I went with my mother!"

He nodded. "I also left her a note on her car windshield, but I guess she didn't read it."

"But that doesn't explain how you connected me to the poem. I could've just gone to the cemetery out of curiosity."

"The night in the library. You and Chrissy and Kevin."

"Yes?"

"I was outside. I followed behind when you and your friend left. I heard you talking. You threw a piece of paper away." He reached into his pocket.

Mr. Theopopolis handed her the paper that bore Kevin's familiar scrawl.

"You took it out of the litter basket?"

He nodded. "I wanted to know what you knew. It seems you're no closer to solving the mystery than I am." The old man shook his head.

Something troubled Angela. She hesitated for a moment before blurting it out: "What were you doing by the grave that first night?"

"I go there all the time," he said slowly. "In the spring I tend to the weeds. On summer nights, when everyone is away on vacation, I sit there for hours by myself."

"But why?"

"Because it's a way to be close to my mother and brothers," he said softly.

Angela felt very sorry for the old man and wished she could help lessen his pain.

"They died here in a fire, in a house that used to be down the path, on what is now the tennis courts. I was only two years old, and my father had taken me into town that day to get the mail."

Angela was reluctant to ask, but she knew she had to. "Is it true he just disappeared one day?"

Mr. Theopopolis said, "Yes. The story I was told is that he went out on the lake and his boat overturned, but I suspect differ-

116

ently. I think my father, who loved my mother very much, was consumed with grief and simply dove into the water and drowned."

"How do you know? You were very young."

"The headmaster, Mr. Hilly, took me in and raised me. He had known my parents many years. He told me."

Mr. Theopopolis reached into the magazine rack next to his chair and produced an old, thick volume which he opened and handed to Angela.

The page bore a picture of a white-haired, mustached man in a dark coat holding a walking stick.

"That was my adopted father, Mr. Hilly."

Angela glanced at the straightforward face. "He looks like a nice man."

"A prince! After I graduated from Glencora he sent me to the university in Maine where he had relatives. They became my second family. After college I drifted around the country. Mr. Hilly died when I was in my senior year. One winter I hitchhiked up here from Florida. I wanted to visit the graves. As it turned out, the school was in desperate need of a history teacher. Here I am, thirty years later."

Angela wished she could say something to

erase the sad memories. But words failed her.

He sensed her mood and attempted to raise her spirits. "I've had a full life, Angela. I have no regrets."

She felt better but still had to get to the core of the mystery.

"Why did someone dig up the grave?"

"To follow the poem. You're familiar with the line 'The graves will shake and spill their dead.' "

Angela knew it only too well.

"Were the graves here when Ambrose Blue was a student?"

"Yes. Mr. Hilly, knowing how my mother had loved the mountain, had suggested the burial in that secluded spot." He faced Angela, not averting his eyes. "Four nights ago the graves were undisturbed."

"Why would anyone go through all this to destroy the school? It doesn't make sense!"

"We're not dealing with a rational person. Remember that. This person is seriously disturbed."

Angela forced herself to ask the one question she feared.

"How much time do you think we have?"

"Maybe none at all," he replied.

Fifteen

On the eve of the school play Chrissy sat in the cramped audiovisual room folding copies of the school paper. The Christmas semester break would begin after the play, and it was traditional to distribute the Christmas issue of *The Glencora Reporter* as students departed.

The front page was devoted to the holiday plans of the faculty and a story on the chess match, announcing that the school had raised $2,078.13 for its building fund. A small but prominently displayed item announced that Selena's father had made a generous contribution of ten thousand dollars.

Chrissy was sorting, folding, and stapling when Angela burst into the room and quickly locked the door behind her.

"What's wrong?"

"Mr. Theopopolis wants to see us right away, and he said to bring your notes and the graph."

"I don't have time. I have to get all this work done," Chrissy protested.

"Bring it with you, we'll do it there. We'll meet in his house. Wait ten minutes and take the path behind the rec hall. Make sure no one sees you."

"I was planning to meet Norman. We were going to go into town for a pizza," Chrissy moaned.

"Norman will have to wait," Angela said. And then softened her voice, "I'm sorry, but we really need you."

Chrissy nodded. "Okay."

"See you soon," Angela said, and left quickly. Angela was secretly happy that Chrissy had finally found a boy to be friends with. She had noted a new glow to her friend in recent weeks and now realized the source. She hoped that Norman wouldn't be angry with Chrissy for canceling their date and decided that somehow she would have to make it up to her.

Chrissy reached for the phone on the desk and dialed the freshmen boys' dorm. One of the students answered the pay phone and Chrissy asked to speak to Norman. She heard the student drop the phone and go off to find him.

Chrissy's palm started to sweat. This was all new to her. Having a date was new—breaking a date was unheard of. She told herself it would be a true test of their friendship, but she was worried she'd fail the test.

"What's up, Chris?" the bright voice greeted her.

"How'd you know it was me?"

"X-ray vision," Norman replied as Chrissy laughed.

"I'm sorry, Norman, but I can't meet you for a pizza tonight." She held her breath.

"Why?"

"Angela wants me to help her with something. I couldn't say no. It's very important."

"Life and death important?" he asked briskly.

"In a way . . . yes."

"Anything you can tell me about?"

Chrissy's voice shook. "I can't."

"Okay." He sighed.

"Norman," she said softly, "I was really looking forward to it. I really wanted to go."

"Yeah. Well . . . Since it's the last night before school ends I guess . . . Well, I was looking forward to it too."

He truly sounded disappointed. Chrissy broke out into a large grin.

"It's okay, Chrissy. Thank you for calling me," he said dejectedly.

"Good night, Norman."

"Good night."

She hung up the phone and stared at it for a long moment reveling in the realization: "He really does like me!"

Chrissy gathered up her materials and hurried from the room. Fifteen minutes later, she and Angela were sitting on the floor of Mr. Theopopolis's parlor with their papers spread in front of them.

For the next hour they examined the chart, made notes, constructed a new chart showing how often certain people were linked to others, and then concentrated on those with a known grudge against the school. Chrissy noted uncomfortably that Mr. Theopopolis headed that one particular list.

The notation had not escaped his notice. "I guess, from an objective point of view, I would be a prime suspect," he said with amusement. "Good detective work." He resumed plowing through the books on his lap.

"Not much to go on here," Angela moaned, after riffling through the old yearbooks.

"It has to be here somewhere. We're just not seeing it," their teacher insisted. "We have to keep looking! If we're on the right track, the person has no choice but to strike tomorrow night."

Chrissy gasped. "What!"

"The calendar year ends tomorrow night, when everyone leaves for the holiday. It'll be January and into a new year when the school reopens. The person has to strike tomorrow night!" the old man said convincingly.

"But," Angela protested, "the poem doesn't mention a specific year. The school year doesn't end officially till June. They could wait till then."

Chrissy jumped up. "Hold it! It does say specifically. The poem says a 'mere fourscore.' That's eighty years, right?"

"Right," Mr. Theopopolis answered.

"But we don't know when the poem was written. He never copyrighted it. It was found in a notebook in the attic years later. It's impossible to know when it was written."

The teacher took a faded piece of paper from his pocket. "It was written exactly eighty years ago," he said, handing them what turned out to be a yellowed, torn copy of *The Glencora Reporter*.

"I came across this last night. That's why I

asked you both to come over. When I read it, I realized how little time we have."

"Read it aloud," Chrissy told Angela.

Angela held the delicate paper that she feared would snap into pieces with the slightest pressure.

"In a previous issue of *The Glencora Reporter* we were delighted to announce the exciting discovery of a poem written by our illustrious alumnus John Ambrose Blue. At that time we asked any former students or teachers who had knowledge of the poem to help us determine the date of authorship.

"Now our search is over. A letter from India, where a former student now resides as a State Department liaison, has pinpointed the date of authorship. We reprint the letter here for your consideration:

" 'Dear editors of *The Glencora Reporter:*

" 'Your last issue, which reached me here in today's mailbag, announces the discovery of John's poem and your desire to ascertain when it was written.

" 'I am happy to report that I can answer your plea. I was fortunate to have shared living quarters with John for a year while I attended the school. I kept a diary at the time, which I'm happy to report is still in my possession.

" 'A specific entry—now before me—reads: "Tonight after military drill, as I was preparing for bed, John came into the room and sat on my bed and read me a poem he had just written about the school. It had to do with a fire and graves and what sounded almost like the end of the world. I advised him against handing it in to the English professor. Too violent, I felt. He agreed."

" 'The date on my entry reads Nov. 13—' "

Angela let the paper slip from her hand.

"Exactly eighty years ago," she said softly.

Chrissy stared at the paper. She remembered the words that had been scrawled on the wall—"The end is near"—and she shuddered.

"Let's get back to work," she said.

Walking back to the Neely house later that night, Angela and Chrissy had to admit reluctantly that the evening had proved fruitless. Their brains were numb from figures, dates, histories of the staff—all of which amounted to nothing. Even Mr. Theopopolis had to admit he was stumped. The mystery's solution was nowhere at hand.

As they approached the cottage, their eyes to the ground and lost in their own thoughts, a figure leapt from the darkness. They spun around in terror, to find a smiling Norman, bearing two pizzas and a six-pack of cola.

"Dinner is served," he announced, holding open the door to the house.

Sixteen

The campus bell rang throughout the mountain, signaling the dinner hour. Students, parents, and faculty members strolled to the dining hall from all directions, and the air was filled with excited chatter. Even the presence of April's mom, wearing a silver mink coat, and Selena's father and his royal entourage, went practically unnoticed amid the hubbub.

Carmela and Dixie had arrived early to spend some time with the Neely family, to thank them for having boarded Angela. Dixie had given Mrs. Neely a black pup from Smokey, the firehouse mascot, who had had a litter of six. It had been a surprise arranged by Angela, who had learned that the woman wanted a puppy.

Mr. and Mrs. Norseworthy stood at the entrance to the dining hall greeting the visitors as they arrived.

Carmela and Dixie found themselves sharing a table with King Elizzaroes, his two military officers, and Mr. Theopopolis. Chrissy and Angela had been excused, as they had to get into costume for the play.

Midway through the meal the king toasted Mr. Theopopolis: "To teach history is an honored profession."

The old man smiled and returned the toast: "To respect history, and heed its lessons, is a greater accomplishment."

An hour later, with all the students, parents, and teachers seated in the auditorium, the curtain rose on Angela and Chrissy dressed as old women. Carmela smiled and nervously reached for Dixie's hand.

"She's going to be great," he assured her.

As the play progressed, the audience settled back to enjoy the zany comedy.

Halfway through the first act, Carmela suddenly noticed that Dixie was not laughing. She felt a slight tenseness in the hand that held hers.

Carmela glanced up at him and noticed he was looking toward the rear of the room.

"Anything wrong?" she asked.

"I'm not sure," he said, as he looked about the auditorium.

"What is it?" she persisted.

"Nothing," he said, patting her hand. "Watch the show."

Angela padded happily across the stage as she prepared to poison her twelfth victim with the arsenic-tainted wine.

The audience, caught up in the antics of the play, shouted at the man not to drink the wine.

Amid all the laughter and cheering, it took the audience a full minute to realize that Angela was no longer acting. She was standing at the lip of the stage, screaming at everyone, "GET OUT! GET OUT!"

Dixie fled from his seat, leapt on the stage, and pushed Angela and Chrissy into the arms of the first row spectators.

He yelled, "FIRE!"

Orange flames licked at the hem of the curtain as Mrs. Norseworthy, her clothing ablaze, staggered onstage. Dixie tackled the woman and extinguished the flames as the audience screamed and ran like a thunderous herd to the exits.

Thick smoke rolled into the auditorium as bodies crashed into each other and chairs toppled. The lights died.

"Angela! Angela!" Carmela cried, stumbling through the crowd that pushed against her. The stage was impossible to reach. She felt two arms grip her tightly and lift her in the air, toward the exit. She fought, clawing and kicking at the air. "My daughter! I have to get my daughter!" The arms held her tighter and carried her out the door, where she was swept upstairs by the fleeing mob.

Outside in the night air, some people dropped to the ground gasping for air while others raced about looking for their relatives. A young man lay moaning, holding his twisted leg.

Carmela heard fire sirens coming up the mountain, but they were too late: a deafening roar filled the campus as flames shot through the roof of the building. Golden sparks flitted through the sky like lightning bugs in a frenzied dance, and people ran and crawled from the explosion.

Carmela fell to the ground sobbing. It was there that Dixie and Angela found her.

"I'm okay!" Angela cried, gripping her mother tightly. "I'm okay!"

Carmela clutched her daughter to her chest. Then she watched in horror as Dixie dashed back into the flames.

"No! No!" she yelled after him. "Somebody stop him! Stop him!"

The fire engines barely came to a stop before the uniformed men jumped off the truck and ran toward the burning building. Carmela gripped the rubber raincoat sleeve of one of the men, screaming "There's a man in there! You have to save him!"

The fireman brushed her aside and barked orders to his men before plunging into the thick smoke.

Angela knelt on the ground next to her mother and hugged her tight.

Seventeen

Driving back to the city the next afternoon, Carmela sat in the backseat of the car reading the headline story aloud to the other passengers.

"Two buildings of the private school Glencora were destroyed last night in a five-alarm fire. Officials are investigating the possibility of arson.

"Police are investigating reports that the fire was ignited by Millicent Greene, 28, a teacher at the school, who perished in the fire. No motives have been ascribed.

"Although the auditorium was filled to capacity at the time of the explosion, no one else was killed. Mrs. Amanda Norseworthy, wife of the school's headmaster, suffered extensive injuries and was admitted to Parkside General Hospital with second- and third-degree burns. Her condition is reported as satisfactory.

"Faculty members Jed Hart and Grace Dixon were hospitalized for smoke inhalation. Robert Brownlow and Janine Ives, students at Glencora, were treated for cuts and abrasions, and Sidney Kubly, the father of a Glencora student, was held for observation after complaining of chest pains.

"Firemen commended the speedy actions of a visiting New York City fireman who was in the audience at the time of the fire.

"According to police reports, interviews with witnesses indicate that Miss Greene acted alone. Her body was removed to the Newburgh City Morgue."

The newspaper front page also included pictures of the fire, with a credit line to Kevin Neely.

"I still can't believe it," Carmela said. She was still weary from the many hours spent at police headquarters while Angela was being questioned.

"How's the arm?" Angela asked Dixie, who sported a cast from his wrist to his elbow.

"I'll be ready for spring training," he

grinned. His face bore a deep, red gash where a piece of wood had glanced off his forehead. Because his clothes still smelled of smoke, he was wearing jeans and a sweater borrowed from Kevin.

"She must have been a very unhappy young woman," Mr. Theopopolis said from behind the steering wheel. "How tragic to die like that."

Chrissy stared out the back window, lost in her thoughts.

Only Mrs. Portnoy, who was sandwiched in between Chrissy and Carmela, seemed animated.

"The story I heard this morning is that Milli and Mr. Norseworthy were close friends when they were at the university in Georgia. He was married at the time," she said, a hint of reproval in her voice.

"She was obviously mentally disturbed," Mr. Theopopolis said. "I don't believe for a moment that there was anything wrong in the relationship. I think they were friends and then when he came here to be head-master he offered her a job out of friendship. I think she manufactured the romance in her own mind."

"Nonetheless," Mrs. Portnoy said, "he's a ruined man. The school will have to let him go. It can't tolerate such a scandal."

"I was in the room when the police were

questioning him," Dixie said. "The story is just as you said," he told the old man. "He felt sorry for the young woman, and when she wrote asking for a job he helped her get it. She tried to make more of the situation, and one time he bluntly told her that he was happily married and would never leave his wife. He thinks that's when she decided that the only way to have him was to get rid of Mrs. Norseworthy."

"She's going to be all right, isn't she?" Angela asked.

"In time," Carmela nodded.

"But he's so old," Chrissy said. "Why would Milli be interested in him?"

Mr. Theopopolis looked in the rearview mirror and smiled. "Even the old can inspire love. Besides," he grunted, "he's younger than I am, so I suppose that makes me ancient."

"But where did Mr. Shulte fit into all this? He was engaged to Milli," Angela pointed out.

"There's no doubt," Mrs. Portnoy said, "that the young man cared for her very much. My feeling is that she used him. Either to try to make Mr. Norseworthy jealous or to divert suspicion from herself. All of them, actually, were victims of her deranged fantasy."

"And what about the graves? Did she dig them up?"

"Probably. But we'll never know for sure."

Angela leaned her head against the car window and gazed at the trees whizzing by outside. Snow was falling softly and a thin coating covered the woods.

She knew she would never forget the sight of Milli, in the blue cape, pouring the can of gasoline over Mrs. Norseworthy and throwing the match.

Angela had seen the hem of the cape catch a spark and ignite into a ball of fire, enveloping the teacher.

It was a sight, she knew, she'd never forget.

She also knew she had a long battle ahead of her to convince her mother to allow her to return to the school.

"I sent you to Glencora so they could protect you while I worked nights and I almost lost you. They won't get a second chance," she vowed.

But what Carmela didn't know was that Mr. Theopopolis, after spending his Christmas vacation in Greece, planned to visit the restaurant and plead for Angela's return.

It was also arranged that Kevin would drive his parents into the city and coincidentally drop by the same evening to add their votes.

Angela felt confident they would pull it off; after all, her mother was certain to be in a great holiday mood and the fire would be but a memory.

For what Carmela didn't know was that prior to the play Dixie had taken Angela aside to show her the engagement ring he planned to give her mother Christmas morning.

"Guess I'm sort of asking your approval" is how he'd phrased it.

"You got it," she had squealed.

Now, driving home, gazing out at the DEER XING signs, Angela wondered what was the proper dress for the daughter of the bride.